The Perfect Catch

The Perfect Catch

A Texas Playmakers Romance

Joanne Rock

TULE
PUBLISHING

Dedication

For Lisa Saunders, who made time to show me some Hill Country highlights during my trip to Fredericksburg, Texas. Thank you so much for spending an afternoon with me!

Prologue

CALVIN RAMSEY HAD experienced some surreal moments in his career as a professional baseball player.

Getting drafted in the first round and snagging a signing bonus that a wise investor could live off for decades.

Playing for half a season with one of his brothers in the minors before reaching the bigs, where he would don the same number his father wore as a pitcher in the major leagues.

Advancing his team in the playoffs with a walk-off homer two years into his career.

He wasn't an everyday starter, but he'd been a difference maker. A utility player who could fill in at five positions admirably, and provide some pop off the bench with a clutch pinch-hit.

But this afternoon, seated in the sports car he'd rewarded himself with after five years in the majors, Cal wasn't sure if he'd ever felt anything quite so surreal as this. He stared out over the half-empty players' parking lot while the guys who'd been his teammates just yesterday were starting to enter the building for another day's work. They would be facing division rivals again tonight, the second game in a week-long homestand. And they'd be suiting up without him.

After arriving at the stadium, he'd been told to report to the general manager's office. And every second since then had felt like an out-of-body experience. He hadn't been sent down to the minors, which considering his slow start and tweaked hamstring would have been understandable.

Nope.

He'd been released. Designated for assignment and put on waivers for any one of twenty-nine other teams to claim. In the weeks to come, he could be picked up by any other team for next to nothing. As of today, he was the special of the week—the player put on the major league clearance rack, so to speak. Though uncertain if another team would pick him up, he was certain that at best his future would be as a journeyman utility guy.

But right now, with his batting average the worst it had been in his entire career, there was a chance he'd be out of baseball for good.

Calvin Ramsey, son of a storied baseball family with a pitching legend for a father, first of his name to lock down a seven-figure signing bonus, had just been given the boot. The kicker was that he hadn't even been remotely worried about his roster spot. He was only a spot starter, but for a half-decade he was a proven commodity off the bench, a fan favorite for timely pinch-hits, and perhaps most importantly, well liked in the locker room. He was the teammate most likely to dump the Gatorade bucket on that day's hero after a win, accepting of his role in the dugout, and genuinely supportive of all his teammates, regardless if their struggles meant more playing time for him.

He'd worked his ass off to gain a roster position. He'd won his arbitration case in the off-season and locked down a bigger contract after a career year. But, as his father always said, it wasn't about what you did last season. A team needed you to perform now. And he hadn't. In baseball, there was always someone younger, stronger and faster ready to take your spot. Cheaper, too. Some wet-behind-the-ears rookie would get his first major league at-bat tonight, courtesy of Cal's hitting slump.

If he sat here much longer, he would hear the sounds of batting practice getting underway. The crack of the brand-new Louisville Sluggers as they launched balls into the still-empty outfield seats. The occasional clink of a ball off the batting cage while the hitting coach worked with someone new on going with the pitch. The usual shouts and ribbing of the twenty-four other…make that *twenty-five* other guys, who were on the field.

Sounds he wasn't ready to hear.

Tipping back against the headrest, Cal couldn't even wrap his head around where to go next. After devoting every summer of his life to baseball since he was old enough to run the bases, he seriously considered just walking away from the game. For good. He'd collect his salary this year either way.

At almost thirty years old, he didn't much feel like jumping through hoops to impress a new team anymore. Maybe he needed to take a summer for himself. Help his grandfather out with the farm that had been in the family for generations—a business doomed to die with the old man since Everett Ramsey's descendants had gone into baseball instead of farming. How many times had Gramp asked him to take over Rough Hollow Farm and Orchards?

It was too soon to make that call though. Because underneath the sense of surreal floating around him, Cal was seriously rattled. Right now, he was going to drive home and put his house on the market. Pack up his things and put them in storage since his time in Atlanta was done. After that? He was not the kind of guy to sit by the phone and wait for a call that might not come. There was a good chance he'd toss his phone out the window and just keep driving. His agent would track him down one way or another if any offers came through.

Sooner or later though, he needed to return home. His *real* home in Last Stand, Texas, where a dose of the Hill Country would remind him of his roots. Because in Last Stand, the Ramseys were first and foremost a farm family, most notable because they traced their local heritage back to 1856 when Virgil Ramsey built a home and barn and called it Rough Hollow Ranch.

Cal needed that brand of reality in a life gone off the rails. He just hadn't known how much he needed it until today. For now, he shut down his phone because he damn well wasn't ready to talk to anyone. Or maybe it was to prevent himself from seeing any sports news about his career going down in flames.

Turning over the engine, he cranked the tunes and lit out of the parking lot like his ass was on fire. He had a house to sell. And, in time, a life to resurrect once the wrecking ball finished tearing down the old one.

Chapter One

My oldest son may stop by the house sometime this spring.

SEATED ON THE porch swing at dusk, Josie Vance reread the text message thread that had sent her into panic mode earlier that week. Ever since she'd taken the job as a caretaker for this mammoth old farmhouse in Last Stand, Texas, she liked sitting outside to watch the fireflies come out as a reward for a hard day's work on the property. At those times, she could almost forget this place didn't belong to her. Like the fluffy little dog on her lap—Kungfu the Maltipoo—and the two Lab mixes snoozing at her feet, the things around her were borrowed pleasures. But when the world all around her was quiet, she simply enjoyed it and didn't care that it was temporary. All week she'd been too frazzled by her employer's messages—the threat of an "oldest son" stopping by—to enjoy the usual twilight ritual.

He has been out of touch, so I can't be sure. It's just maternal intuition!

Hailey Decker, the author of the texts and the home resident who'd hired her, was an unusual sort of woman to say the least. She was divorced from a famous ballplayer, apparently, some pitcher that Josie had never heard of. After her divorce, Hailey had moved back into the first home she'd lived in as a married woman, a place next door to her ex-father-in-law, because she still looked out for the older man, Everett Ramsey. That had been Josie's first indication that Hailey was unique. Because who moved back into a house long owned by a divorced spouse's family, let alone cared for an ex-in-law? Add to the mix that Hailey was a local bee-keeper who thought nothing of dropping everything to lead a church mission to Ecuador for three months or going mushing with a team of sled dogs in Alaska for a winter holiday, and you came up with an intriguing human.

Tucking her bare toes under her on the worn green seat cushion, Josie cupped her mug of tea tighter in response to the cooling breeze that came after the hard spring rain that had driven her indoors late that afternoon. Just now, as she listened to the katydids sing, the crickets chirp, and the swing gently creak, she could almost convince herself that her employer's texts had been all for naught. Despite Hailey's "maternal intuition," Josie hadn't seen any sign of the sons around the property. Which was just as well since she needed to be anonymous for a while. When she'd agreed to the caretaking gig, she'd signed on for overseeing the house, the dogs, a cottage garden and several beehives.

Strange men showing up at the house had not been mentioned.

If you see Calvin, please mention he is welcome to stay with his ailing grandfather. Thank you!

Josie set the phone down again, hoping she never saw the mysterious Calvin for a variety of reasons, but also because she knew Everett Ramsey was hell-bent on looking out for himself. The cantankerous old farmer next door had been sideswiped by a tourist bus a month ago and was lucky to be alive. When he'd first come home from the hospital, Josie had hardly seen him. But over the last two weeks, she'd spotted him outside using his walker on the pitted dirt road that separated his place from hers. He swore a lot about not being able to do as much as he used to, and when she tried to assist him, he'd sworn even more about the nurses who paraded through his house night and day like he was an invalid.

They'd reached a reasonable peace when Josie discovered she could help him if she distracted him with farming questions. When Everett thought she needed his help, he was far more gracious about accepting hers. She was having fun getting to know him, in fact. And he'd invited her to sell some of Hailey's peaches at the Rough Hollow Orchards farm stand next weekend, insisting Hailey would want her to keep the money since she'd be doing all the picking herself.

Josie looked forward to that. And she didn't feel like sharing her new friend with an outsider grandson who hadn't been bothered to come home before now. She needed the peace this place offered to overcome a betrayal of trust that had left a significant dent in her confidence.

She closed her eyes and breathed in deep, focusing on the

scents of a world washed clean around her so she could ignore the anxiety she felt about anyone imposing on the peaceful haven she'd found in Last Stand, Texas. She felt safe here.

She'd ignored her instincts the last time a stranger came calling—back in her old life, where her mother laughed at her for having too many "irrational fears." She'd let herself be wooed by a handsome swindler who sweet-talked his way past her defenses, and painted a picture of a life for the two of them on the other side of the globe, where they would protect the whales, clean the waters, and make fish safe again. He hadn't realized how thoroughly ready she'd been to escape her life in the first place, and the daily strain of working for her emotionally unstable mother.

But the money and the man both vanished the moment she'd clicked "send" at Western Union. The local news outlets who'd gotten wind of her folly all agreed she'd fallen for a classic con. Her naïveté had made for a handful of entertaining headlines in her Florida hometown. She was a cautionary tale now. A caretaker for three months because she had nothing left of her own.

Not even her job, since her mother had fired Josie from the work she'd done—for a pittance—since she was a teen, acting as property manager for the low-income housing building her mom had inherited from a relative. The job had always put Josie between a rock and a hard place with tenants who needed things fixed and a building owner who refused to invest a nickel in repairs. She'd wanted out of that position for years, and that had been the real reason she'd risked everything to trust the swindler. She'd seen the life he offered her as a better option. And when her mother realized how serious she'd been about leaving the job, all hell had broken loose.

In her tirade, her mom had threatened to turn Josie in for doing contracting work without a license. Grossly unfair, considering her mother had been the one who'd always told her to find a way to fix things herself if she wanted better conditions for the tenants. But Josie looked up the penalty for that kind of charge, and it could be serious.

Although right now, she was a world away from all that stress and anger. She'd bought a new cell phone and no one knew where to find her. She hoped, in time, the argument would blow over.

Sipping her cooling tea from the dark brown stoneware mug, she stroked Kungfu's fur and reminded herself she was okay. Sure her bank account was empty, but she was free now. Away from the toxic relationship she had with her mom. On her own, she could experience perfect moments like this one—seated on a porch swing after a rainstorm, counting fireflies while the moon rose high.

Still, she hoped the universe didn't test her any more this year. Because she really, really wasn't ready to deal with a stranger showing up at the door.

LONG PAST MIDNIGHT, Cal slid his key into the back door of the old country farmhouse where he'd been raised. A house now occupied solely by his mother since she'd divorced his dad and vacated the over-the-top mansion Clint Ramsey had built after retiring from baseball. Like his siblings, Cal felt far more at home here, next door to his grandfather's farm, on the property where Ramseys had lived since Last Stand became a town.

He'd driven straight to Last Stand from the airport in Houston once he'd made his mind up to come home after spending the last two weeks in Mexico. Only one of them sober.

Since he'd never been a drinker as a professional athlete, he'd felt entitled to all the tequila he could handle to toast the end of his career. He'd cleared waivers and remained unclaimed three weeks after he'd been designated for assignment. Barring a miracle, he was out of baseball for good. Now, stepping silently onto the braid rug inside the kitchen, he was just about to help himself to whatever leftovers were in his mother's refrigerator when the barking started.

Deep-throated woofs mingled with high-pitched yaps. Nails scrambled on hardwood as the race was on to see who was at the door. Cal cursed himself for not remembering that his mother kept a pack of dogs around at all times. So much for not waking her.

Would any of the mutts remember him from the last time he'd visited her here? Two years ago, he guessed.

Probably not when he hadn't recalled them either.

The pack descended the stairs and skidded around the corner, a little tornado of white fluff leading the way. Two excited Lab mixes galloped behind it. Relieved his mom hadn't taken in any super protective guard breeds, he relaxed a fraction.

"Take it easy, guys," Cal cautioned them, extending a hand for the bigger dogs to sniff while the little one alternated growling and jumping. "Put a sock in it and I'll share whatever I find in the fridge."

The Labs sat attentively the moment he reached for the handle of the stainless-steel refrigerator, their tails wagging in almost perfect synch. The fluff ball darted between his feet as if it wanted first peek at what was inside.

Perplexed at the almost completely bare shelves, Cal tugged open all the empty drawers and heard a floorboard creak overhead, not surprised the racket had woken his mom.

He stared at the quart of strawberries and bundle of asparagus, both clearly picked from her garden. He couldn't recall a time in his life when he'd shown up at his mom's house without a homemade pie or bread lurking somewhere. A leftover soup or pasta dish. A container of cookies in the freezer.

"Damn." He scratched the littlest of the dogs on top of her furry head while the animal stood with her paws in the base of the barren wasteland masquerading as a fridge. "Either Mom's been abducted by aliens or she's selling this refrigerator."

Tipping the door closed, he heard an ominous metallic click behind him, followed by a hoarse feminine voice.

"Turn around slowly," a woman who was not his mom rasped. "And show me some identification or I'll call the cops."

Cal peered behind him while the dogs defected to the newcomer's side.

Because there, standing behind him with an ancient .22 caliber rifle pointed at his chest and wearing his mother's bathrobe, was a woman he'd never seen in his life. Dark hair stuck out from her head at all angles. She looked young and possibly hot, but his brain drew boundaries at anything wearing his mother's robe.

Also, his grandfather's hunting rifle deterred normal male thoughts.

"Who the hell are you?" he demanded, lifting his hands over his head since that felt like a more natural response to a gun in his face than digging for his ID.

Besides, the woman shook like a leaf as if she was the terrified one even though she was holding the weapon. He figured he'd better not make any startling moves or he'd end up with a hole in him. Possibly worse.

"I might ask you the same thing!" Bright blue eyes wide, she lifted her head from the scope to glare at him.

He suspected—whoever she was—she had no earthly clue how to use the .22 if she'd been employing the scope while he stood roughly eight feet away from her.

"I'm Calvin Ramsey," he shouted louder than he would

13

have liked, but he was exasperated, starving, unemployed and being held at gunpoint in his childhood home. "Where's my mother?"

The dogs all barked in response, for all the good that did him.

"You're the oldest son." The woman seemed to have some sense of recognition then.

She tipped aside the stock, *thank you, God*.

"That's me." He began to lower his hands. "I'd like to put my hands down if you can maybe set the gun down?"

"Um." She stared at the .22 as if surprised to see it in her hands. "Okay." She bit her lip. "Hailey won't appreciate hearing that I greeted you with a rifle. But I had no idea you might let yourself inside while I was sleeping."

Reaching for the .22, he gently took it from her, all the while trying not to hear sexual innuendo in words where clearly she'd meant none. But the exasperation, starving, and unemployed bits all still conspired to make him surly and raw. He emptied the chamber of the rifle and pocketed the ammo for good measure before he rested it in a corner of the kitchen.

Without the gun in her hands, he had new appreciation for how hot she was—robe be damned. He was pretty sure she was naked under the yellow terry cloth splashed with purple flowers. Petite and curvy, her feminine body had pin-up appeal while her face was full of sharp angles. A narrow nose that pointed at the tip. Precise blades for cheekbones. Dark, perfectly straight eyebrows.

14

"My mistake," he agreed with as much chivalrous good humor as he could manage at one in the morning. That said, he didn't have a scrap left to continue making small talk. "Now, who are you and where's my mom?"

She pursed her lips and cocked her head at him. Miffed. Instead of answering, she reached under the sink cabinet and retrieved a bag of dog treats. The restless canines lined up as if there was an award for best posture. She doled out the biscuits and tucked the bag away again.

"I'm Josie Vance, the caretaker," she announced slowly, lowering herself into one of the wooden chairs around the kitchen table. She withdrew a cell phone from her pocket and placed it face down in front of her.

Her words sent a jolt of panic through him.

"Caretaker for who? Is Mom okay?" He'd disconnected his cell phone for the better part of the last two weeks to avoid dealing with the fallout from his career. It had never occurred to him something could happen to someone he cared about in that time.

He took a seat across from her while the dogs sprawled out underneath them.

"Hailey is in Ecuador, leading a church mission to build a school." She sounded proud of this, her chin tipping up. "She hired me to take care of the house, dogs and bees. And the garden. And I'm sure she asked me to relay something to you, if I can just find her note."

Relieved, he propped his elbows on the table, watching Josie flip over her cell phone to scroll through her messages.

"Ecuador?" He mulled that over, regretting that he didn't know this about his mother.

He'd been too caught up in his own drama this spring, hiding out from the sports news, unwilling to hear how they'd painted him in the press. He'd done a damn good job of avoiding the world, too. But obviously he'd missed some big things.

"She doesn't communicate often since she has to make a special trip into town for connectivity." Josie Vance the caretaker spoke with the kind of clear articulation that he associated with a kindergarten teacher. A very hot kindergarten teacher. Her gaze returned to her device. "But she said if her oldest son stopped by, to tell you that..." She stopped scrolling to read aloud. "If you see Calvin, please mention he is welcome to stay with his ailing grandfather."

Alarm surged along with a blast of anger. She couldn't have told him that first? He swore. Twice.

"What's wrong with Gramp?" His head throbbed. Not eating before he came home had been a mistake. He needed to power up his phone and find some food.

Josie arched one of those very straight eyebrows of hers. "According to him, everything. But he's out of the hospital now and doing amazingly well for a man who was hit by a tour bus a month ago."

"A tour bus?" He swore some more. Why the hell hadn't his father informed him? "Like in a collision? What was he driving?"

Fear for his granddad squeezed his chest for a moment

until he reminded himself that she said he was back home now. Recovering.

"It sounded like the bus grazed him while he was walking to a neighbor's birthday party in downtown, I think. Most of the damage was done in his effort to move out of the way."

Couldn't one of his siblings have found a way to get that news to him?

Or his father, the only other person in Cal's family currently living in town?

"You do bear Everett a strong resemblance," she said cryptically before giving him the highlights of the accident and assuring him that his grandfather was already out walking daily. Then she passed him her phone. "Maybe you should read the local paper. I know there has been news coverage about the accident. You could get up to speed that way."

"Thanks, but that's okay. I'll unearth my tablet and get caught up tonight." He slid her offering back across the table. He'd dated women for months who wouldn't let their phone out of their sight for more than ten seconds at a time, let alone share it for his personal use.

There was something different about his mother's caretaker.

"So." She peered at him hopefully. "You will stay with Everett?"

"About that." His brain hadn't even made the leap yet, but obviously she didn't want him to crash in his old room for the night. "I actually don't have a key for his house."

She nibbled on her lower lip again. A gesture he might not have seen as erotic if she had more clothes on. Or if he hadn't been starving, tired and etcetera.

"It is after one a.m., so I hate to startle Gramp in the middle of the night," he pointed out. "And my room is on the opposite side of the house from the guest room. You won't even know I'm around."

She drew a breath as if to argue. Then, leaned forward slightly, her blue eyes narrowing.

"If I agree, perhaps we could not mention to your mother the little mix-up with the rifle?"

"Deal." He reached to shake on it, pleased by how fast they came to terms.

And, as his hand enveloped hers, he was unexpectedly turned on by the soft feel of her. He helped himself to a tiny stroke along her knuckles before he let go and called it a night. He'd go to bed hungry—that was for damned sure. But for the sake of sweet dreams about a woman who hadn't once mentioned baseball...

It wasn't a bad trade at all.

Chapter Two

S LEEP PROVED IMPOSSIBLE with a strange man in the house.

Josie had checked and double-checked Calvin Ramsey's face against the framed photos of him in Hailey Decker's dining room—family pictures from long-ago Christmases and ski trips. Sure, the man who'd been standing in front of the refrigerator had been older and surlier than the boyish face in the photos. But there'd been no denying the resemblance. The Ramsey men had all been blessed with absurdly good looks, and Cal in particular, as far as she was concerned.

Which was why she'd spent the night too restless to sleep even behind the locked guest room door. Josie knew her own weakness when it came to a handsome face. The one time in her life she'd made a truly rash decision, she'd been egged on by an attractive man. And the swindler hadn't possessed nearly the swoon factor that Cal Ramsey did.

So she rose at dawn, determined to carry on in her caretaker duties the same way she had before he arrived. Hard work settled her nerves and gave her a sense of purpose. Plus it meant less time to ruminate. She'd been struggling to keep deer out of Hailey's garden this week, and in the process she'd let the weeds get ahead of her. She could fix that today.

She had blisters on both hands by the time she heard the screen door slam on the main house. Sweat poured in a steady stream down her back thanks to the Texas sun. The wide-brimmed straw hat she wore was as much a staple of weeding as the hoe in her hands, but the hat was old and ill-fitting, poking her forehead through the worn lining.

Her surprise housemate looked none the worse for wear, however. Cal Ramsey strode down the back steps with a coffee mug in hand, his green eyes surveying the big back-yard and the cottage garden that took up almost half of it. With his brown hair still damp from a shower, and the scruff shaved off his face, his rugged good looks were even more obvious. On most men, the deep scowl on his face would have been unattractive. But Cal wore a touch of hostility as well as his jeans. Which was to say, to damnably good effect.

"Good morning," she said amiably, hoping to avoid new drama, no matter what was eating at him.

She returned to hoeing a row of yellow squash, careful not to tangle the tool in any of the long vines that spilled over into the bean patch.

She'd planted more marigolds and sunflowers to try and deter deer, but she could see signs of them tromping through the bean plants.

"It's after noon," he informed her. "Shouldn't you take a break?"

"I'm okay." She was a bit thirsty, actually. But she had

hoped to work outdoors until he vacated the premises.

"You don't look okay. You look ready to drop from heat exhaustion." Stalking closer, he sounded even surlier than when she'd greeted him with the rifle. "I think you've weeded enough for one day. You should come inside and have something to drink."

She stopped chopping a particularly long root and leaned on the hoe like a walking stick, caked dust crumbling off her gardening glove.

"I'm from Florida. The heat doesn't bother me and I know all about proper hydration." She really thought he would be long gone by now so she could return to the peace of her pre-Cal days, carefully reassembling her life and her dignity in the quiet anonymity of Hailey Decker's farmhouse.

Unfortunately, she couldn't expel him with the same efficiency that she'd tackled crabgrass and tree roots. A mosquito whined near her ear and she fanned it away.

"You're from Florida," he mused as he bent down to twist the nozzle on the hose coiled near the back steps. Her gaze greedily followed him, his every movement a study in athletic grace. "How did you find out about a caretaking job in Texas?"

He dumped the water from the dogs' water dishes and ran a cool stream through them from the hose. She happened to know the Labs were snoozing in the dirt under the porch, but Kungfu roused herself from her spot and padded out to take a drink.

"Your mom posted the position online." She toed aside an overflowing bucket of weeds she'd pulled, the green leaves already wilting in the hot sun. She was unprepared for an inquisition when she was thirsty and—she now realized—ravenous.

She'd been weeding for hours, thinking she'd have breakfast once her guest left the house. Who'd have known that wouldn't be until after noon?

"And you decided a temporary job in Last Stand sounded like a fun way to spend the summer?"

She bristled. "It seemed like a good opportunity to see another part of the country. Does it matter?"

"My mother is a soft touch. She likes to take people at face value and trust her gut when it comes to hiring help." He stared at her over the brim of his coffee mug as he lifted it. "Me, I like background checks. References. That sort of thing."

"I'm hardly a felon." She also couldn't argue much about his mom since she'd appreciated Hailey's faith in her good character. Josie hadn't trusted her one and only work reference—aka, her mom—not to throw her under the bus based on their fiery parting.

"Excellent news." He sipped his coffee while her stomach growled. "You're out of creamer, by the way. And sugar. And everything else."

She was actually surprised he'd found coffee. She'd thought she'd finished off the little she'd scavenged from the pantry. But she was exceedingly grateful for a timely change of topic.

"Who needs sugar when there is an abundance of fresh fruit and vegetables?" She gestured to the garden around her, remembering how much money she was saving by not visiting the grocery store. "And Last Stand has an interesting history, by the way. I was excited for the chance to spend some time here."

"A historian *and* a health nut," he mused, his scowl easing while he badgered her. "I'll have to be careful not to bring around any pie from Char-Pie so I don't tempt you unnecessarily."

"Pie? I'm a healthy eater, not a masochist." She was suddenly hungry enough to march into the nearby orchard and start tearing peaches off the tree, but she didn't want to let him know he was getting to her. "I would be offended if you didn't share good pie."

"I stand corrected." He set down his coffee mug on a small outdoor table and sauntered closer, looking cool and composed in the heat that was stewing her alive. "In that case, I'll pick up a pie to thank you for letting me spend the night."

She refused to be goaded by that last comment, however. Even if she itched to set the record straight that she most definitely hadn't *let* him spend the night. She'd been coerced.

He stood close enough to smile down at her. Close enough for her to appreciate the outline of muscle visible under his T-shirt.

23

"How kind of you. Coconut cream is my favorite, in case you were wondering." She hadn't had a taste of white, refined sugar in weeks. The honey the local bees made was good. And the fresh fruit was amazing. But nothing quite took the place of good, old-fashioned cane sugar.

"You haven't tried Char-Pie's French silk."

She shouldn't think about French silk and this man in the same conversation. Besides, he was surely just teasing her to get a rise out of her. To get under her skin. She might have once believed that swindler Tom Belvedere had been interested in her, but even *she* wasn't gullible enough to think this very hot, very self-assured, gorgeous man was flirting with her.

Some men just couldn't turn off that mode. It was how they related to the female world.

"I'm not picky." She repositioned the hoe so it stood between them, accidentally fanning a light spray of dirt over their shoes when she moved it.

He glanced down at his Italian leather loafers and then back up at her, his green eyes narrowing a fraction.

"If you went into town with me, you could see the selection for yourself," he suggested easily. "I can't help but notice you don't have a vehicle of your own, which makes me wonder—"

"No. Thank you." She pivoted on her heel and headed toward the potting shed to put her gardening gear away. "I've got lots to keep me busy here."

She couldn't afford to spend any more time with him

when he clearly enjoyed prying into her life, asking too many questions. She was afraid he might hound her further about her past or her plans. Or ask her about references and experience she didn't have. But before she reached the potting shed, she spied his grandfather up the dirt road that divided the two properties, pushing his walker over the pitted path.

"There's Everett," she announced, pointing behind Cal. "He'll be glad to see you."

And, just like his surly relative, he swore twice.

"I'll be back later to get my bags," he warned her, the scowl returning now in full measure. "We can talk about why you don't have a car, or groceries, or a bathrobe of your own."

"I have my own bathrobe!" she shouted after him, though she doubted he heard her since he took off toward his grandfather at an impressive run. With any luck, Everett would keep him too busy to follow up on that conversation, because Josie had depleted her stall and diversion tactics for one day. The last thing she needed was for Cal Ramsey to start digging around in her past and potentially cost her the job at his mother's house for the summer.

When Hailey Decker had hired her, Hailey hadn't cared that Josie had no experience. Or references. But the truth was that she had both—she simply hadn't wanted to share the details for fear her previous job would sink her chances of working anywhere else. Technically, she'd been fired because her mother had been angry with her—not for falling prey to a con per se, but for attempting to spend her money on an effort to leave home for good.

Of course, Josie's mother had "fired" her in the past when she was angry. That usually amounted to docking her paycheck for a week to demonstrate displeasure about Josie siding with a tenant in a dispute, or calling in a contractor to fix something without her mother's approval. Not this time.

So who knew what Cal might find if he decided to look into her past? A bad reference and lack of experience at the minimum. But the possibility of legal charges still loomed if her mother pressed the case with the local authorities. For now, she would just have to work harder. And send Hailey lots of photos of the thriving, nicely weeded garden, assuming she could keep the deer away from it. But first, she was going to devour a massive lunch of whatever produce could be washed and prepped as fast as possible before her next encounter with her boss's too sexy son.

"GRAMP, SHOULDN'T SOMEONE be helping you?" Cal asked a few minutes after greeting the older man. He squinted into the sun toward his grandfather's house, regretting that he hadn't made some calls about Everett's health when he first woke up.

He'd slept late, his first good night of sleep in weeks, and then he'd gotten entirely too distracted watching Josie attack the weeds in his mother's garden as if she had a personal vendetta against anything that touched the squash plants. He'd never seen anyone wield a hoe with as much force as the caretaker, especially given her size. For someone with such sweet curves, she had oddly gangly arms and legs, thin and tanned. And no wonder given there wasn't a stitch of food in the house.

What was up with her? He'd puzzled over it far too long when he should have been getting the scoop on Gramp's health from one of his brothers or even—worst-case scenario—his father. Cal had been avoiding his dad's calls ever since he'd been released from the team, not ready to hear Clint Ramsey's take on things. His relationship with his father was…complicated.

"I don't need help," his grandfather replied, gnarled hands clutching the walker tighter. He wore a bathrobe over a T-shirt and cotton pajama pants, although he'd taken the time to put on real shoes with good soles for walking. "Bad enough I have to use this contraption everywhere I go."

He steered the walker's wheels back toward his own house at Cal's urging. He couldn't afford to get distracted by Josie anymore today, and this way, they were walking away from her, the garden, and the house where Cal grew up.

"I read a little about the tour bus accident online." He'd stayed up well after he'd tangled with Josie in the kitchen, trying to get up to date. "I'm sorry I didn't come home sooner."

"I don't need babysitting," Gramp assured him. "Never have."

"Was Dad around at least?" Cal pressed, knowing his sister was traveling the globe while his brothers were both still busy with their own seasons. Nate was sick of bouncing between Triple- and Double-A, while Wes was killing it in Triple-A, expecting a call-up soon. "Has he been checking on you since you've been back home?"

"He comes over most days." Gramp shook his head, his white hair lifting in the breeze. He'd lost a fair amount of weight since Cal had seen him at Christmastime. "But he's not a lot of help with the farm, as you well know, and that's what I really need right now. Someone to be my eyes and ears around the place. For all I know, I'm paying too much for that manager to muck things up."

Gramp listed sideways like a boat blown off course, his feet following the walker when it hit a high patch of grass. Cal tried to reroute both of them onto a flatter part of the dirt road.

"I'm sure he's doing a good job, Gramp. Dad vetted the guy carefully."

Gramp made a disgusted sound but didn't comment.

It had been a big conversation two years ago when Cal's grandmother had passed away. Everett had been grieving and upset and lashed out at all of them for not stepping up to help with the business. Cal's father had finally talked Gramp into hiring an outside manager to oversee what was left of the farming operation and orchards since Gramp had been adamant he didn't want to sell any more of the farmlands that would one day go to his grandkids since his own son had never wanted any part of it.

Cal had never thought he'd have any interest in it either since, up until a few weeks ago, baseball had always been his life. Now?

He still couldn't see himself as a farmer. But he had an abundance of time, and he owed his grandfather some help.

"I can check in on the business this week," he ventured. "If it would put your mind at ease."

What he really wanted was to spend more hours with Gramp and make sure he was healing, but if what mattered most to his grandfather was a scouting report on the farm, Cal would figure it out.

"You'd do that?" Gramp stopped the walker, turning to glance up at Cal.

He looked sort of misty-eyed too, and Cal hoped he was just tired. Still, it gutted him to think that something so small mattered so much to his granddad, and that Cal had never given it any thought until right this minute.

"Hell yes, I'll do that." He dropped his arm around Everett's shoulders and urged him forward, ready to get them both out of the heat. "But keep in mind, I know exactly nothing about orchards and farming, so you'll have to tell me what I'm searching for."

"You know more than you think," Gramp assured him, nodding with satisfaction. "You didn't spend every day of your youth on a baseball diamond, son. I took you out to the farm plenty of days when you and your siblings were little mites."

Cal didn't think that driving a hay wagon or feeding calves were going to be useful skills anymore, especially now that Rough Hollow had gotten rid of all their cattle. But he didn't mention it since his grandfather seemed pleased for the first time.

"Then I'll wander around the place tomorrow and tell you what I see." Cal pointed toward the historic house that looked a little worse for wear. It needed paint, first of all. A temporary ramp he'd installed a few years ago for his grandmother appeared warped in places too. And there was a handrail loose. "Today, I'm going to make a run into town for groceries." Along with paint, lumber, and of course, pie. "You've got some bulking up to do."

"Bah." Gramp made an impatient gesture with his hand, his body weight falling forward enough to have Cal scrambling to keep him upright.

He figured since his grandfather didn't follow up the protest that equaled to Cal winning the point.

"After I get back from shopping, I'd like to move a few of my things over to your house. That is, if you don't mind me staying with you for a little while."

"I don't need babysitting," Gramp reminded him, steering the walker around a rotten board on the ramp as they neared the back door.

"I realize that, but with Mom in Ecuador, I can't exactly crash with the caretaker."

Gramp stopped midway up the ramp. Cal couldn't believe he wasn't sweating bullets by now, especially with the robe on over his pajama pants.

"She's a pretty girl." His grandfather peered up at him, as if looking for confirmation of the obvious. "Hard worker, too."

"A pretty girl who made it clear she's not in the market for guests." Cal mopped his forehead, wishing they could get inside where there was air conditioning. "So if it's just the same with you, I could use a place to stay—"

Gramp was already shaking his head.

"No?" Cal was stunned. And offended. "What do you mean, no? Oldest grandchild means nothing to you now?"

"The apartment over the garage is better for a young bachelor." Gramp lifted a gnarled finger to make his point, forcing Cal to grip him tighter again. "Your mom renovated it a few years ago and toyed with the idea of renting it out again."

The garage apartment hadn't occurred to him. His parents had used the space for rental income in the early years of his father's career—before Cal was born. The extra money had helped out before his dad's contract negotiation for the money that bought them the big house on the other side of town.

The idea had appeal. Except it would make it that much tougher to help his grandfather.

"I'm not sure I'll be able to find the key," he hedged. "And If I stayed with you, it would be easier for me to make repairs around here. The house needs some work and some paint."

"Nonsense." Gramp pushed the walker forward. "Come over anytime. And this way, you can keep an eye on the pretty girl, too."

He was incorrigible. But then, infernal stubbornness came with the last name.

"You know, I do okay with the ladies on my own," he felt compelled to remind him as he opened the door to the mudroom. "Even when you're not around to give me suggestions."

"Men don't always know how to choose the right girl."

Cal severely missed his grandmother right then. Marlene Ramsey had always been the most skilled at arguing with Everett, especially when he started spouting opinions about the female persuasion. A pang of grief for his family caught him off guard.

"Is that so?" he played along, knowing he wasn't going to win the argument anyhow.

Besides, he was feeling more compliant now that the air conditioning hit the sweat on his skin. Although he'd be willing to guess the thermostat was probably set around eighty degrees. Not exactly arctic cool.

"Absolutely. Look at your father. He chose well the first time and the second? Bah." His grandfather dismissed the idea of Brittney Ramsey with a shake of his head, then headed toward a chair in the living room. "You should take the young lady to the orchards with you tomorrow."

"I'm not sure Josie knows any more about fruit trees or farming than me." Cal saw out the front window of the living room that a car had pulled into the horseshoe driveway with the name of a health care group painted on one side.

He was relieved to know someone was checking on his grandfather. He got him settled in a chair near a table with his water pitcher, newspaper and television remote.

"The girl's got a green thumb!" Gramp protested. "Have you seen your mother's garden since the new caretaker arrived? And she's great with the bees. Ask her what she thinks the bees can do on the farm. I have hives for the orchards, but Hailey told me I should use some on one of the crops. I can't remember what one."

"I'll text Mom," Cal assured him as the doorbell rang. "I think one of your aides is here."

"There's no law that says we have to answer it," Gramp grumbled. "And your mother can't receive texts in Ecuador except for once a week. Ask the pretty caretaker about the bees, for pity's sake, son. I'm doing all the work for you."

Cal opened the door to a perfectly nice nurse's aide and then left her to speak with his grandfather while Cal inventoried the kitchen and the shed. He wouldn't bother Josie with questions about bees and crops after she'd exhausted herself weeding. If he wanted to annoy her, he'd ask her why she didn't have her own vehicle and what she was trying to accomplish by doing without something so fundamentally important out here in the country, miles away from town.

For tonight, he'd content himself with finding the key to the garage apartment and then getting out of her hair.

He had a lot of supplies to buy and plenty of tasks to

keep him busy for a few weeks so he didn't dwell on the fact that his baseball career was over.

Having Josie around as a pleasant distraction was just icing on the cake. Or, in this case, pie.

Chapter Three

I T HAD TAKEN great restraint not to do an internet search on Cal. Josie had spent the afternoon picking, washing, chopping and storing extra fruit and veggies so she had more variety prepped for meals. She had a few extra bushels of peaches that she could sell at the farm stand too, if Everett's offer for her to do that was still open. All the while, she'd wondered about Hailey's oldest son, and what kind of career left him free to come and go through Texas, but without a home. His car looked crazy expensive, as did his clothes.

Curiosity was killing her, but if she gave in and searched his name, it would be the first step in admitting too much interest. And that was exactly what she was trying to avoid after she'd been conned, duped, and parted from her money by the last charming guy she'd met. So every moment she had enough discipline to deny her curiosity about Cal was a source of personal victory.

She'd been doing a check of the apiary after a supper of early tomatoes and grilled peaches when she spotted his exotic-looking convertible parked on the dirt road where Everett liked to walk. She took as much time as she dared around the bees, preferring to wait until Cal had retrieved his things from the house before she returned to an outdoor patio where she'd been reading a book. But bees didn't appreciate having their routines interrupted, and she didn't need sulky bees withholding honey, so she finally headed back toward the patio table tucked under what looked like an old pole barn converted into an outdoor dining shelter.

The poured concrete floor was covered with an all-season rug, a fan spinning lazily from the open rafters above. Behind the wrought-iron table, a narrow bar and barstools were flanked by a full-sized refrigerator on one end and an ice maker on the other. Both were unplugged and empty for the season, but Josie could imagine how pleasant it must be to have parties here, especially when the perennials peaked. She was about to drop back into a seat at the table and read until it was dark out when she heard the screen door slam on the main house.

Cal strode down the back steps from the house, wearing a different pair of expensive-looking jeans from this morning. Another tee that fit his very well-made body in a very appealing way. He wore scuffed boots now, however, instead of the loafers.

"Any idea where my mother would keep a key to the garage apartment?" he called across the small patch of lawn separating them.

Was there such a thing? Her gaze darted to the garage on the opposite side of the yard, noting it was indeed two story. And resided very close to where she worked every day.

"I... Um." She'd had high hopes of putting more distance between them than that. "Not specifically. But there is a cabinet full of keys just inside the basement door."

"I'll check there." He wandered closer to her covered retreat spot, his boots stirring the grass that needed mowing. "And for what it's worth, my grandfather is a hard sell for a roommate."

"Unusual behavior for a grandparent." She found it tough to scavenge all the prickly defensiveness she'd felt earlier around him. It would be easier if he went back to needling her about her past. Or her eating habits. "Were you so very bad as a child?"

He threw his head back and laughed. A startling sound. When he met her gaze the next time, his eyes were a hint greener. Mischief danced there.

"Most definitely. But I think it has more to do with his fear that I'll cramp his style." He stood closer to her now. Near enough to make her remember how attractive she found him.

She resisted the urge to remind him Everett would benefit from having someone keep a better eye on him. From how fast she'd seen him sprint to help his grandfather earlier, she guessed he already knew that.

"In that case, the garage apartment is a good compromise," she told him honestly, fighting the urge to step away from him. It would be better for his grandfather to have a relative close by. As for the fact that it would put Cal in close proximity to her, she'd work on an avoidance strategy. She'd had an opportunity to hone that skill in her work for her mother since she'd either been ducking bill collectors or impossible-to-please tenants most days.

He studied her for a moment, frowning. "You're handling a new neighbor better than I anticipated."

"You're the boss's son. I'm not sure it would help my career prospects to complain."

"Are you planning to go into caretaking permanently, then?"

"I like keeping my options open." She felt her defenses sliding back into place. "Do you want me to help find that key?"

"No, but I could use some assistance with another task."

She resisted a sigh, thinking the universe had put him in her path to test her. And to keep testing her.

She just needed to be strong. To focus on his words and not be swayed by his very green eyes or his outsized attractiveness.

"You'd like to eat healthier?" she guessed, not letting her eyes wander over his already perfect physique.

"Definitely not." He spun away from her to stroll around the covered patio area. He peered inside the empty outdoor refrigerator. Glanced at the cover of the book she'd been browsing. "*Balanced Beekeeping*?" He read the title aloud like a question.

"I found it on your mother's shelf. It's about living in better harmony with bees."

He gave her a side-eyed glance, his voice suspicious. "Did you know anything about bees before you took this job?"

She folded her arms. "Can we get back to whatever task required my assistance?"

"It's about bees, actually." He hooked a hand in the rafter overhead. Tall people could do that sort of thing. It was fortunate there was a table underneath the fan or he could have hit his head on it. "My grandfather thought it would be a good idea for you to visit the farm with me and see if any of the crops could benefit from the hives."

His broad chest took up too much space. Too much breathing room. He was much too distracting. But as she skittered back a step, she was able to let his words sink in. About his grandfather wanting her opinion.

"Really?" She'd spoken with Everett briefly about the bees and Hailey's garden, mostly to distract him while she helped him back to his house that first day. "He wanted my input?"

"Yes. Though in all honesty, I think he was angling to set me up." Cal shrugged his shoulders, lowering his arm.

"I'll let him know you're not my type," she returned distractedly, already thinking about the possibilities of seeing a big farming operation like Rough Hollow Orchards.

If she had a job prospect in Last Stand after Hailey returned from her trip, it would save having to buy a vehicle, something she had no way of affording. Plus, she'd liked Hailey in the brief amount of time she'd spent emailing with her before she took the job, then their in-person visit where she'd learned the ropes of caring for everything around the property. It would be nice to start over somewhere she already had a sort-of friend.

"So you're considering coming to the farm?" Cal prodded, clearly surprised.

"Absolutely. I picked some peaches from your mother's orchard that I need to drop off anyhow." She returned to her book and sat in the chair, knowing she didn't have many hours of daylight left to read. Also, she needed the barrier of the book between her and this man who got under her skin far too easily. She cracked open the hardcover volume to the page with a bookmark. "But I'd better return to my beekeeping manual if I want to bring my A game to the farm tomorrow."

She studiously avoided his gaze, trying to focus on the words but not even seeing them.

"I'll send a truck over to pick up the peaches since I don't have room for bushel baskets in my car."

"Fine. Thank you." She flipped an unread page. "But I'd still like to go to the farm."

"You realize I'll have all day to ask you questions?" he needled.

She smacked the book back down in exasperation. "Are you trying to scare me off?"

"No. Just being honest. You haven't exactly been forthcoming about what brought you here."

She took a gamble and a shot in the dark, hoping to deflect his questions. "For that matter, neither have you."

"I *live* here," he protested a bit too loudly.

Maybe her shot in the dark wasn't too far off the mark.

"In your mother's house?" she pressed, suddenly curious about what had brought him here in the middle of the night. Clearly he didn't live around here or he would have gone to his own place.

His gaze narrowed. "It's still my hometown."

"And I still have quite a few questions of my own, but you don't see me badgering you about them."

He tilted his head. "Are you implying you'll badger me tomorrow if I make polite inquiries about you?"

"I'm suggesting we call a truce to focus on farming."

He huffed out a long breath and didn't seem in any hurry to leave. "It doesn't sound as much fun your way."

She almost cracked a smile. And, realizing how close a call that had been, she promptly turned her attention to her bee book.

"Just for a day. Just long enough for a farm visit," she told him from behind the safety of the cover.

Thankfully, he was already on his way back to the house to look for the key.

She would figure out how to deal with her hot neighbor for a few hours if it meant a chance to make herself useful on the farm. Or to learn something that might catapult her into her next job opportunity since—unlike Cal—she most definitely wasn't interested in returning home.

THE NEXT DAY, Cal rose early to fit in a workout since old

41

habits die hard.

Or at least that's what he'd told himself. His phone might not be ringing with offers, but his agent had gotten in his head the night before with a text telling him to stay in playing shape because he had a few "irons in the fire" about Cal's future. Probably just a tactic to lift a struggling client's spirits. Yet the words had gotten to him, reminding him he'd been lax on training since being released. And the trip to Mexico hadn't helped.

But after he'd finished a long run, then cleaned up his younger brother's weight set in the garage to pound iron until his arms shook, Cal knew the fierce workout wasn't related to baseball or old habits. Mostly, he wanted to tire himself out before spending the day with a woman who tempted him too damned much.

The sexy caretaker next door was intent on keeping secrets, and Cal wasn't sure he trusted her. In his world, women who kept secrets were the kinds who hid the fact that they were married in order to have an affair with a ballplayer. Hell, his own stepmother had latched on to Cal's father with a similar ploy, tearing the family apart and breaking Cal's mother's heart. Not that it was all Brittney's fault. The lion's share of that blame firmly belonged to his father. But the incident had made Cal plenty wary.

He could watch out for himself, of course. But he worried about his mother, who still trusted too easily. How thoroughly had she looked into Josie Vance before hiring her to live in her home for months?

Stepping outside after a shower later that morning, he spotted Josie on the wraparound porch. She wore a short-sleeved, gauzy white tunic over a pair of jean shorts with cowboy boots. Her dark hair was woven into a short braid, a blue ribbon tied around the tail. She carried a small cloth sack from the local food co-op under one arm like it was a handbag.

And damned if all the working out had done a single thing to take the edge off when it came to her. Attraction flared, hot and fast, making him realize he was only fooling himself to try and fight it. If he wanted her this much, why not simply get close to her? It wasn't like he'd be sticking around Last Stand forever. Sooner or later, he'd get back on track with his career, if not as a player, maybe he'd investigate his prospects as a manager. Baseball was his life.

As she rose from a wooden porch rocker, she frowned at him, opening her mouth to speak. Cal cut her off, having a good idea why she was unhappy with him today.

"Good morning." He nodded in the direction of his convertible that he'd left in the driveway after his errands the day before. "Are you ready to go?"

"I am." Her jaw jutted. "But honestly, Cal, I can't accept all the groceries you bought."

He liked squaring off with her, liked feeling the sparks they generated off of one another. Maybe this new plan to follow the attraction was going to work out perfectly well. He'd stay close to her, and keep his mom safe at the same time. Whatever secrets Josie was hiding weren't going to hurt him.

"Mom will appreciate having her kitchen stocked when she returns." He opened her door for her.

"She told me just the opposite—that I should finish anything in the pantry since she likes to shop when she comes home."

"Does she?" He didn't bother closing her car door since she hadn't slid inside the vehicle yet. He headed around the front to get in his own side. "Then help yourself to anything. It's not like I can return groceries."

He turned over the engine on the BMW i8 while she begrudgingly took a seat beside him. "You shouldn't have bought so much."

"But on the bright side, at least you had enough coffee to go with the pie." He put the vehicle in reverse, liking the hint of her scent he caught as he glanced back over one shoulder. "Was I right about the French silk?"

He glanced down at the stick shift and ran an appreciative gaze over her thigh that was almost within touching distance. Was the fixation with her a result of leaving baseball and not having enough to occupy his brain? Or had it simply been too long since he'd found time to date? Of all the women he could have chosen, why was he so damned taken with a mystery woman who'd made it clear she didn't want to get to know him better? Today's "truce" was proof of that since they'd agreed to not ask each other questions.

To just let it be.

Something he'd never been very good at. Drive, determination and outright stubbornness were the secret to his success.

"The French silk was amazing. But I thought the coconut cream that I tried for breakfast this morning was every bit as good." The hint of bliss in her sigh lit a fire inside him. "But it begs the question—how did I end up with a half pie of each? Do they sell half pies?"

"No. I bought two pies and divvied them up. I gave the other half of the coconut cream to Gramp, and kept the other half of the French silk for myself, leaving a whole pie for you."

"Your grandfather needs to bulk up and you're clearly a man who can afford a lot of calories." The once-over she gave him was damned flattering. "Yet I'm the one who ended up with the most pie?"

"I call that Texas hospitality since you're the newcomer to Last Stand." He gave the vehicle gas as they reached the county route that ran along the south side of town, enjoying the smooth acceleration of the high-end sports car. "But if you have trouble polishing it off, I'm right next door."

"I'll manage somehow." There was a hint of humor in her voice, as if she wanted to be amused but couldn't quite allow herself to have fun with him.

Because she was scared to get close to him? Worried she'd let something slip about the past she didn't want to talk about?

He couldn't help wanting to see her smile, no matter what she was hiding. He might be wary of her, but she'd clearly made an impression on his grandfather, and that counted for something in Cal's book. He liked knowing that Josie was concerned for the older man, enough to keep an eye out for him when Everett went for walks. She couldn't be all bad.

"So what do you want to see today?" Cal asked as he slowed down for a truck with a horse trailer in front of him. "I'm going to the Rough Hollow roadside stand first, which is close to the main barns and the manager's office. Once we're there, we can take one of the trucks or utility vehicles to check out any of the orchards or crops."

"Ideally, I'd get a list of everything you grow, then I can research while you drive so I can tell you the things I want to see. The only thing I know for sure I want to check out are the hives."

"Do we need bee gear for that?" The wind in his hair helped air out the tension that had been knotting him up since he'd come home—worries about his mom, about Josie, about Gramp.

Convertibles were good that way.

"Definitely not. Although we might want to save that stop for later in the day when the bees are calmer."

"I feel like, as a matter of personal safety, I should at least have some sense of your bee experience." He glanced over at her as he turned into the parking area for the roadside stand.

Her eyes were on the building in front of them, surrounded by a half dozen cars, and decorated with hay bales, hanging pots of flowers, and bushel baskets of peaches.

Beneath the simple décor, the Rough Hollow Farm and Orchards sign needed painting, and the whole building was in worse repair than his grandfather's house. It ticked him off to think his father had done so little to help out in the last few years. It was one thing to be unwilling to go into farming. But would it kill his dad to offer financial support to the business that had been in the Ramsey family for over a hundred years?

"This is so charming," Josie announced. "It looks like it should be in a magazine. A slice of Americana." She turned bright blue eyes on him, excitement lighting up her whole face.

Over what, he wasn't quite sure.

"It's seen better days." Although Cal had been avoiding his father, it became clear to him now he would have to make a visit to Clint Ramsey and plead his grandfather's case.

If the Ramseys were going to keep Rough Hollow, they needed to take better care of the business.

She peered over at him and then back to the business. "It's a farm stand. It's not supposed to look like a Whole Foods."

He would have argued the point, but she was already opening her door to check out the place.

Too late, he realized that his sports car was on the flashy side for Last Stand. A few people milling around the peach baskets were now looking his way, openly curious. Cal swore at himself for becoming a baseball cliché, because this was exactly the kind of stunt his father used to pull, and Cal had always hated the added attention that his dad seemed to enjoy.

Stepping out of the BMW that had drawn stares, Cal could see one of the bystanders whisper to his kid—a boy of about ten years old wearing a ball cap of Cal's former team.

Way to go, Ramsey.

He wasn't in a good headspace to make the appropriate remarks and tell the kid how hard work paid off, or how grateful he was to be in the big leagues since—of course—he wasn't anymore.

And he felt plenty bitter about it.

"Calvin Ramsey?" The boy approached him with a grin while his father stuffed a pen into the kid's hand.

The hubbub drew Josie's attention from where she sniffed a trailing vine of white flowers spilling out of a hanging basket. Her blue eyes darted from the kid to Cal and back again.

Missing nothing.

So much for keeping his career quiet.

As soon as Josie spied the boy whip off his baseball hat and pass it to Cal along with a pen, the pieces fell into place.

Cal was a famous baseball player.

She remembered his father had been a pro pitcher. And there'd been a reference to "baseball-playing sons" in her emails with Hailey Decker about the job. At the time, Josie had assumed Hailey referred to scholastic athletes and younger kids, and she'd promptly forgotten all about it in a rush to impress the woman with her knowledge of bees and gardening.

But it came back to her now, and it made sense that Cal was built like a pro athlete, because gauging by the awed hero-worship in the boy's eyes as Cal signed his hat, Cal *was* a professional athlete. He also had the ease with money to buy a sports car and treat strange women to a pantry full of groceries.

Although, she wondered as Cal shook hands with the kids' parents, what was he doing home during the spring when the baseball season was already underway?

She hated to be any more obvious about her eavesdropping, but she was fairly certain the boy's father had asked Cal about his team. She wandered closer, picking up the occasional peach to cover her movement.

"...one day at a time and we'll see what happens," Cal was saying with a forced geniality that didn't sound quite right coming from him. Or maybe it did. She'd just never heard that tone from him before. Like a radio station suddenly playing a different kind of music. "There's always next season. Nice meeting you."

There was hand shaking and back clapping all around, followed by a group selfie before the young family got into their pickup truck and drove away. Leaving Cal and Josie in the farm stand with an older couple currently paying for a small basket of cherry tomatoes.

Cal's eyes met hers and she only had a second to decide her course of action.

But as curious as she was, she intended to honor the truce. Mostly because she needed him to quit asking questions about her past. Besides, if he was a pro ballplayer, he'd be leaving town soon enough for the sake of his career, wouldn't he? She didn't follow professional sports, but she guessed maybe he was hurt and on a leave of absence or something. She would just have to remain patient.

"So how do we go about finding the beehives?" She busied herself with admiring a display of blueberries.

She didn't glance up when he didn't answer right away. Instead, she moved on to a bin of melons. Deliberately casual.

"I'll ask," he said. "The manager's office is in back."

As his footsteps retreated out of the store and to—she assumed—the big barn behind it, Josie wondered if the clerk would have a list of the crops grown on Rough Hollow lands. Now that the farm stand had emptied of everyone except for the two of them, she hurried to the counter to ask.

The clerk was texting a mile a minute. The girl looked like summer help—late teens at the oldest, but more likely a high school student. She had platinum-blonde hair tinted blue at the tips.

"Excuse me." Josie cleared her throat after a minute when the girl's thumbs didn't show any inclination of slowing. "Could I ask a question?"

"Of course!" the girl said in a cheery voice, her focus still on her phone screen. "Just texting my friend that I saw one of the Ramsey brothers. She'll die when she hears. She loves the Atlanta Rebels."

"The who?" Josie figured she had a few minutes before Cal returned. She could ask a question or two.

"The Rebels?" the teen repeated more slowly, as if that would help. She set her phone on the worn wooden counter by the electronic tablet resting on a cash drawer. "The team that cut him earlier this season? I mean, I'm not a big baseball fan like her, but the Ramsey brothers have a cult following here because, well. You know."

She grinned and shrugged like they shared an inside joke.

"I'm not from around here, actually," Josie clarified, keeping a sort-of watch at the corner of the farm stand in case she saw Cal's long shadow returning.

"Oh, right," The clerk's gaze went to her phone that buzzed three times in quick succession. "Rough Hollow is owned by the Ramsey family. Mr. Everett is still in charge since his son, Clint, went into baseball and then, all of his grandsons went into baseball and the granddaughter…well, she left Last Stand long ago. Cal's been in the majors the longest, and I like, *never* see him around here even though I've worked here since last fall."

So Cal had been keeping secrets from her—of sorts. Or had he assumed she knew about his family full of athletes? His job explained the expensive car and clothes, the body toned like a machine, maybe even the wariness that dogged him. She imagined pro players were hounded by hangers-on who wanted to be a part of their world for selfish reasons.

But not her. She'd prefer to put ten paces between herself and anyone who was remotely famous. She needed to avoid the spotlight at all costs until the trouble at home died down.

The phone vibrated three more times and the girl burst into laughter. "Sorry!" she apologized to Josie. "I knew Darlene would go nuts when she heard." She picked up the phone and flipped it over, eyes scanning fast. "She wants a picture? Oh God, how can I get a picture?"

Josie figured she'd lost her audience, but since the coast was clear, she couldn't resist asking one more question.

"You said he got cut this season?" she asked, wanting to be sure she'd understood. "As in, lost his spot on the team?"

The clerk nodded. "It was so awful—"

"Josie, let's go." Cal's voice startled them both as he came through a back door on the opposite end of the store.

She scrambled back from the counter while the teen dropped her phone. Josie hurried past the blueberries and melons to the archway where Cal now stood, his expression stony.

Had he overheard her question? Guilt swamped her even as she kicked herself for not being more careful.

"Ready," she announced brightly, peering past him into the greenhouse that connected the barn to the farm stand.

"Are you certain?" His voice was low, just for her ears, before he took her hand and tugged her into the greenhouse behind him.

A fan whirred overhead, conditioning the air that smelled like potting soil and growing things. He tipped a metal door closed behind them. A door that closed silently and reminded her how thoroughly he'd startled her when he re-entered the store.

"Absolutely." She wanted to say it with conviction. To move on and see the beehives. But her heart was beating too fast with him holding her hand.

And standing too close to her.

His green eyes probed hers, his nearness making her recall his very intriguing male physique. Was it really her fault she felt a flare of feminine interest when he was a professional athlete and had the body that went with it?

"Make sure you know what you're in for, Josie, before you say yes." His voice lacked the geniality that she'd heard him use with the young baseball fan. It was all gritty-edged and hard now.

And did something wicked to her insides. Something she couldn't allow herself to feel so soon after another man had deceived her.

Nerves made her blurt the first thing that came to mind.

"I signed on for beehives." She'd been very clear about that from the outset, hadn't she?

Cal released her hand, but he didn't back away. "Except now you've broken our truce by asking questions. So in return, I've got a few questions of my own."

Chapter Four

"**I** DON'T KNOW what you're talking about." Josie looked right into his eyes and lied to him.

Even if he hadn't overheard her asking the store clerk about his situation with the Atlanta Rebels, Cal would have recognized the falsehood because of the way she rushed the words out of her mouth.

"You're a terrible liar," he informed her, fuming mostly with himself for bringing her with him today, for driving her here in his convertible that looked more at home in the team parking lot than in Cal's small Texas hometown.

Was it any wonder they'd drawn stares?

Not that it even mattered she knew about his career or that he'd been cut by the team. Big deal. He'd known she'd hear about it eventually, but he'd been enjoying the anonymity of being with her. Of being a regular guy.

"You're right." She caved quickly enough, the humidity of the greenhouse already pulling dark curls from the braid where she'd tried to tame her hair. "I *do* know what you're talking about, but you're wrong about me breaking the truce, since I didn't ask you a single question today."

She had the audacity to look self-righteous about that. It

might have had something to do with the way she pressed her lips together.

He debated kissing the expression away. Slowly. He could see the way the pulse at the base of her throat throbbed, her nerves all too obvious. Because of him and the thread of attraction that connected them? Or because she didn't want to reveal anything about herself? He guessed he'd better press his advantage now and work on that kiss later.

A disappointing decision, he acknowledged. Especially when the humidity of the greenhouse intensified the hint of fragrance emanating off her skin.

"You didn't have to ask me anything," he reminded her, trying his best to keep his eyes off Josie's mouth as she stood backed up to a wall of fruit crates. "You were quizzing the girl behind the counter for all she was worth."

"I hadn't declared a truce with *her*," she snapped. "You can't blame me for being mildly curious when everyone in here gawked at you on arrival, running over for selfies and autographs." She gave him a once-over with her very blue eyes. "You're not *that* hot."

She rushed through that last bit. Even more telling was the way her cheeks turned a shade pinker.

"No?" He didn't want to feel amused. Or aroused.

Unfortunately, he was both. So he canted closer to see the effect he had on that racing pulse at the base of her throat.

It sped faster.

"Definitely not." She swallowed visibly and edged out

55

from between him and the fruit crates, wandering past a bin full of seed packets. "So you can see why I'd want to know what all the fuss was about."

She paced away from him, and he couldn't deny that the long view of her was wholly satisfying too, her toned legs a pleasing sight in what remained of her cutoffs.

"You asked questions, plain and simple. Now it's my turn." His gaze followed the gentle sway of her hips as she strode the length of the greenhouse.

The fan spinning overhead made a gentle *whooping* sound as it sliced through the heated air.

"One question." She pivoted around. Caught him staring.

Busied herself with peering into empty pots stacked on the far end of a worktable.

"Two. First, what really made you decide to leave Florida and come to Last Stand?"

She frowned down at one of the clay pots, running her finger over a chip in the side. "I lost my life savings to a con artist and needed a fresh start."

Definitely not the kind of answer he'd expected, although he couldn't have said exactly what he thought she might say.

"A con artist?" Indignation fired through him. "Did you file a police report? Are they looking for him?"

She remained silent, her lips pursing in a mutinous line as she toyed with a trowel resting on a wooden table.

Frustration knotted his shoulders.

"Okay, don't answer those. But I get a second question, because I know you asked at least two about me—don't deny it," he said, before she could protest. He could tell she wanted to based on the way she drew in an indignant breath. "Second, did you know anything about bees before you took the job watching my mother's house and hives?"

"Beekeeping experience was never a requirement," she shot back, slamming down the trowel. "And no, I knew nothing about it."

"Did Mom know that when she hired you?" he pressed.

"That's three questions." She retied the ribbon around the tail of her braid. A sign of nervousness? A need for order? "Are we ready to go check out the farm now?"

He had about a million more questions, but since he didn't particularly feel like talking about the status of his own life right now, he shoved them aside for the time being. If she didn't know what she was doing with the bees, wouldn't his grandfather see through her? It seemed like a problem that would resolve itself, although kudos to her if she could read a few chapters of *Balanced Beekeeping* and have good advice to offer a man who'd been farming all his life.

"Sure. There's a vehicle we can borrow back here." He pointed in the direction of a side door out to the equipment barn. "I've got a map of the plantings from the farm manager."

He held the door open for her and she passed through, tugging the map from his hand as she stepped outdoors. Cal tried not to make it obvious he was breathing her in, though he may have leaned fractionally closer to catch her scent.

He didn't know what it was about her—a woman with secrets and, he now knew, no money—that drew him like a magnet, but she did just the same. Maybe he simply craved a distraction from the one-two punch of getting booted off his team and not getting picked up right away. It had been a drop-kick to the ego, for damned sure.

No matter the cause behind his new fixation with Josie Vance, Cal found himself thinking about the kiss he hadn't taken back in the greenhouse, and he regretted that now.

The hunger for her only sharpened.

What happened to his plan to get close so he could keep an eye on her? He'd never win her over by sparring with her all the time, questioning her motives and her past.

Leading her around a rusty old John Deere parked between barns, Cal found the Gator, a two-seater utility vehicle the farm manager had told him about. The vehicles were easy on gas and could handle the bumpy dirt roads better than a truck, especially traveling between fields.

"This is us." He pointed it out to Josie and the two of them climbed in, the keys already in the ignition. "Where to first?"

He liked the close proximity of having her in the passenger seat. She leaned forward over the map and one of the white tassels from her blouse fell onto the paper he'd given her. Dark hair slid forward too, more pieces coming loose from the braid. Seeing the way she studied the map of the farmlands, devoting all her attention to the task, reminded him that she was here by choice today. She'd been willing to risk his questions and his company to do something kind for his grandfather.

Had that been part of the job? Cal knew his mother frequently looked in on his grandfather when she was in town. Though Hailey Decker hadn't been born a Ramsey, Everett had always liked her, insisting she move back into the home where she'd raised his grandkids even after she divorced Cal's father. It wasn't out of the realm of possibility that his mom had asked Josie to keep an eye on Everett.

Even if that was the case, she certainly wouldn't have been expected to exert this level of effort to humor the old man.

"Watermelons," Josie announced, straightening from the paper. She pointed to a spot north of the barns. "If we start there, we can circle around and end the day near the hives."

"Fair enough." He turned the key in the ignition and followed the road in the direction she'd indicated.

He could be patient for one more day. See what he could learn about her without asking questions. Although he damn well wanted to know how someone had conned her. She didn't strike him as the kind of woman who would be easily fooled.

They hadn't even passed the big barn yet when she turned to him and said, "For what it's worth, your mother knew I didn't have any firsthand experience with bees."

Surprised she was answering one of the questions he'd

peppered her with in the greenhouse, he gladly filed away the information, keeping his eyes on the road.

Josie leaned back in her seat before she continued, "I emailed her a summary of what I'd been reading to prepare for the job, and she said what she was more concerned about was having someone who wasn't afraid of bees and who was interested in learning about them."

"That makes sense." He pressed the accelerator harder once they drove beyond the barns. The wind in his hair helped cool him down. "I tried messaging my mother last night, but I haven't heard back from her yet."

He wanted to find out exactly what his mother knew about the caretaker she'd hired. If she'd done her due diligence before inviting a stranger into her home for three months. His mom had been through enough after Cal's father had cheated on her. Living in the same town as Clint's new wife couldn't be easy on her either.

Cal planned to make sure no one hurt his mother again, including a doe-eyed brunette with a killer body and secretive past.

"She usually only has service once a week," Josie reminded him, raising her voice to be heard over the noise of the air whipping past them. "I try to send her photos of the dogs and the garden, plus updates on your grandfather. She's been worried about him."

As was he. But he didn't share that thought since his phone vibrated. Even in the bright glare of the sun, he could see his father's number fill the screen for the third time that morning.

Damn it. Chances were his dad was sick of being avoided and wanted to talk to him about being cut. His father would have plenty of thoughts about how Cal had screwed over his own career. But what if he wanted to talk about Everett?

"I should take this call." He steered the Gator over onto the shoulder, the vehicle dipping down on one side with half the tires sinking in the soft dirt alongside the gravel. "But straight ahead is the watermelon field if you want to have a look."

Josie was already stepping out of the vehicle when he connected the call. His gaze followed her as she walked away, her denim cutoffs hugging her hips, inspiring a renewed hunger for that kiss he hadn't taken back in the greenhouse.

He wanted her. And he was going to need her even more after he dealt with whatever his father had to say. One way or another, Cal wanted this day to end with him getting a whole lot closer to the sexy caretaker.

JOSIE COULDN'T BEGIN to guess what had transpired in Cal's conversation with his father. But his frustration with the brief talk had been obvious the rest of the day. He'd tuned out completely for a little while, making follow-up phone calls to other people while Josie toured blueberry and strawberry patches. Cal had been present, but only as a driver while she peered at plants, took photos of fruit and flowers, and quizzed some of the farm workers she'd seen.

Even now, hours later while Cal drove her back to his mother's place, she sensed his thoughts were elsewhere. Maybe it was because her own relationship with the only parent she'd ever known was complicated and frustrating, but she found herself empathizing. The county road wound beneath them as they rode with the top down in his sleek convertible, the buttery leather seats and high-tech engineering oddly out of place in this backdrop of four-rail fences all but buried in tall grass and weeds, crows squawking overhead as the sun sank lower in the sky. Grazing cattle and stubby trees dotted a hillside nearby while a tractor kicked up a thick dust plume in the distance.

"If you see Everett tonight, you should tell him his watermelons would benefit from bees," she ventured, since he hadn't asked for her opinions about the farming operation one way or another.

"You think he should use Mom's hives?" Cal glanced her way, his green eyes lighting with an interest that had been absent for most of the day.

Either she'd found a way to distract him or maybe five hours had finally run out the clock on his brooding time.

"He could rent hives from someone else if he wants." She shrugged. "But it would be easy enough for me to run them over there if I had a helper and a truck. Besides, if the bees don't give him better results with the crop, it's probably just as well if it doesn't cost him anything to try it out."

"Because you're not sure this will work," Cal confirmed,

looking back at the road as they neared the turn for the Decker home.

"Everything I've read makes it sound like this would be a good time for the added pollinating power." Reading was the super power of different girls. It had always given her a confidence advantage to consult books. And if nothing else, books provided an escape when the real world felt too unfriendly. "But bottom line, I can't know for sure if it will make a quantifiable difference in the crop output."

Cal mused over that while he throttled the car back to navigate the gravel road.

Josie hadn't left the property since she'd arrived two months ago, courtesy of a kindly bus driver who'd agreed to drop her off closer to her destination. She'd only been able to afford the bus fare when one of her mother's elderly tenants slipped her the funds after hearing Josie argue with her mom. For that matter, Mrs. Gonzalez had been the one who'd helped her find Hailey Decker's ad for a caretaker, emailing her the link to the job. As soon as Josie had received her first paycheck, she'd sent the money back to Mrs. Gonzalez. She'd been saving the rest, and appreciated the extra cash Everett was letting her keep from picking Hailey's peaches.

Seeing the farmhouse now as they wove down the back road toward the property, she remembered how she'd felt to see the place that first time. Like a homecoming. Or how you wished it felt to have a homecoming. With its sprawl of porches on all sides, the white clapboard house sat between two big hickory trees that kept it shaded. Chimneys and gables dotted the gray slate rooflines of additions that must have housed bigger generations of Ramseys in bygone eras. While not as old as the historic Virgil Ramsey homestead next door—a property that bore the year 1856 on a cornerstone—the farmhouse was over a hundred years old, and was traditionally used as a residence for the oldest Ramsey son since running Rough Hollow was a family business.

To Josie's eyes, though, the place just said home. She could imagine it decorated for the holidays in red bows and green boughs. Or with Indian corn and hay bales at harvest time. It was a house that called for a tire swing and Popsicles, with a yard full of kids.

"It must have been great growing up here," she said wistfully, remembering the way her mother's Jacksonville apartment had felt like a big upgrade from the rickety one-bedroom house in Central Florida where she'd spent her first ten years.

She and her mom had a hardscrabble life when her mom worked in the citrus groves for very little pay, leaving Josie alone for long stretches of time. But then her mom had inherited the apartment building from an aunt who'd died without any children, and to Josie, having her own bedroom had made up for a lot of other things she didn't like about living in a city. Her mother had told her then they'd only gotten the building by luck, and their luck could run out anytime if they weren't careful. Josie had taken her at her word, and—not wanting to return to the citrus groves—she'd spent the next thirteen years doing everything she could to make sure they kept the building running. She blinked away the memories when Cal spoke again, trying to ignore the knot in her belly that thinking about her life in Florida always brought these days.

"Things were good when we lived here," Cal admitted as he drove past the house toward the garage in back. He didn't pull inside, however, leaving it halfway between the main house and the garage apartment. "It was only when my father dragged us all to the mini-mansion on the east side of town that my family went to hell."

He stepped from the car with the same athletic grace that marked his every movement. Josie felt like a dusty, sweaty mess in comparison after poking at plants and earth all day, but she followed him out of the vehicle.

"If this was my house, nothing would pry me out of it," she called over her shoulder as she hurried to the side entrance and let the dogs out. The three barked happy greetings before tearing off into the thicket behind one of the barns, and she noticed that Cal still leaned on the front fender of his car. Phone in hand, his thumbs moved over the screen.

She didn't wish to pry about his family, but she also found it tough to turn away from him if he wanted to talk. So she strode back down to the garden to flip on the sprinklers while she admired the backyard with most of the garden weeded.

There was the converted pole barn with the entertaining space where she liked to read in the evenings. She'd forgotten to switch the overhead fan off last night and it spun on low, now, stirring the wind chimes that hung near the entrance.

The potting shed had been painted white with stencils of bright flowers twining around the green door. A wheelbarrow leaned up against one wall and a silver watering can rested on the stone steps.

With the gentle hiss of the sprinklers watering the garden, she found her attention drawn back to Cal. She walked closer to him, curious why he hadn't disappeared into his apartment yet.

Maybe he wondered the same thing about her. And the truth was she wasn't sure why she hadn't taken cover indoors at the first opportunity. Maybe she felt grateful to him for including her in the trip today, giving her a chance to make an impression on his grandfather or somehow make herself useful to the farm. She really needed more seed money before she could leave here and start over somewhere new.

"I messaged Gramp about the bees," Cal informed her, his phone out of sight and his focus on her. "He gave the idea the green light and said to give you whatever you need to make it happen."

"That's great." Surprised at Cal's easy agreement to her proposal, she hadn't expected him to act on it so quickly. "I can take five hives over, but I'll need a truck to transport them."

She stopped a few feet away from him.

"And someone to help you," he reminded her, straightening from where he'd been leaning on the fender. Shrinking the space between them with just that one movement.

Something about the way he said it sent a shiver of awareness through her. Or maybe it was the way he looked at her.

"Right." She nodded, heart speeding, feeling every inch the awkward girl she'd always been. She was better when they were sparring and circling each other, gloves at the ready. "Maybe one of the farm hands I talked to today—"

"I'll help you." He loomed over her because he was so very tall.

But backing away seemed too much like slinking, and she would not let herself slink. He was far too attractive.

And very, very...fit.

"Sure." She nodded again, and suspected she looked like a bobble-head doll. She forced herself to be still. "Just let me know when you get a truck—"

"I'm free tomorrow morning." His gaze dipped to her mouth. Just for a moment. Then his eyes locked on hers again. "Why don't you let me make you dinner and we'll work out the logistics?"

And that's when she knew he was playing her. The dinner invitation was too much. Was he used to women falling at his feet? Defenses snapped back into place as she saw through his game.

"No, thank you." She released a pent-up breath, grateful to have escaped the seductive spell he could weave around her too fast. Surely she was wiser than that now. "I've got a mixed berry salad calling to me from the fridge."

This time, she did step away, and it didn't feel at all like slinking. It felt like reclaiming her dignity, even if a hint of regret smoked through her at the thought that flirtation might be a reflex for him, and didn't have anything to do with her.

"Care to share it with me?" He lifted a dark eyebrow, his charm still potent even when she realized what he was doing.

"Actually no," she told him honestly, unwilling to be taken in by him. "I might have gone for dinner if I thought for a second you were actually interested in discussing bees or the farm, but I'm not inclined to fall for Casanova moves just because I happen to be single and living next door."

He frowned, folding his arms across his broad, gorgeous chest. "I'm pretty sure I was talking about bees, wasn't I?"

"In between the lothario looks, maybe." She felt her spine straighten and wished she could temper her anger down a notch, but it hurt to think he was toying with her. "Don't forget I just got played by a professional, so I'm once bitten, twice shy. And this is definitely *not* a good time for romance games around me."

"The con artist romanced you?" He sounded genuinely surprised.

"Yes. Although not for long before I wised up," she admitted. Part of the reason she'd come to Last Stand was to heal from all that. To find her own strengths and figure out who she wanted to be. "But I promise you, I'm not an easy mark anymore."

Chapter Five

TWO DAYS LATER, Cal stood on a ladder, rolling paint onto his grandfather's house in the late afternoon. Since Gramp insisted he didn't want anyone hovering over him, doing work around the place was the easiest way to keep tabs on him while he recovered from the accident.

The nap on the paint roller was deep to saturate the porous stonework on the main part of the house. It splattered on him whenever he loaded too much paint from the tray, leaving his forearms frosted white. But the work was satisfying, with the tangible reward of beautifying the historic property. Plus with the view of his mother's garden from this height, the chore allowed him to keep tabs on Josie too, since his effort to get close to her had gone south in a hurry. She was out there now, doing something with the hose. Patching it, maybe.

Funny that he'd learned more about her from her rebuff than he had with any of the questions he'd asked her. She'd lost her savings to a con artist—not through a tricky swindle, but because she'd trusted the guy. At least, that's what he'd gathered by putting together the pieces.

The thought of it made him jam the paint roller harder

into the stone crevices as he worked. He wouldn't mind getting in the car and driving to Florida to find the guy. But she'd drawn a boundary around herself and her past the other night, a line in the sand that only an idiot would ignore. She was prickly about romance and with good reason. Even though the attraction clearly ran both ways, the hot caretaker didn't plan to act on it.

Heard and understood.

Except he'd been a whole lot more disappointed about that than he should be given how briefly they'd known one another. Plus, she thought he'd been playing her, which didn't sit well with him. He may have had an ulterior motive for sticking close to her. But he sure as hell hadn't been faking his interest. So he'd sent over a truck the next day, with a farm hand from Rough Hollow Orchards, to help her with the bees. He'd stayed out of their way, giving her space.

After using up the rest of the paint in his tray, Cal had to descend the ladder to pour more. By the time he stepped off the last rung, he heard voices from the front of his grandfather's house. With his view of the driveway blocked, he hadn't noticed anyone pull in.

Then, Clint Ramsey's too-hearty laugh put Cal's teeth on edge. His father was here. Worse, he had just turned the corner of the house and spotted him. His wife followed him on too-tall heels, her short floral dress and carefully curled hair broadcasting her refusal to fit in to the more down-to-earth world of the Ramsey family. But then, Cal's father was the one who'd turned his back on farming, his own father, and—eventually—Cal's mom, in order to create a different life for himself in the gaudy mansion on the other side of Last Stand.

The betrayal had hurt Cal more than it hurt his brothers. Or at least, he thought it must. Cal had emulated his father. Worn his jersey number through high school and into college before his father's infidelity. Wearing the number as a pro had come with a certain bitterness, but Cal had soldiered onward with it, knowing that fans appreciated the nod to a former idol of the game.

Remembering his phone call with his father two days ago—and his dad's insistence that he would help Cal reclaim his spot on a roster—Cal seriously considered forgetting about the painting project and making a break for his convertible. If he wasn't worried about getting paint on the BMW's interior, he might have.

Dressed in an olive-colored jacket and khaki trousers, Clint Ramsey looked like he'd been styled by the wife almost two decades younger than him, or by an overambitious retail clerk, though the clothes were nice enough. Clint still worked out often and had avoided a paunch, but at sixty-four years old, he had the leathery skin of a man who'd spent every waking moment in the sun. He wore his now-silver hair the same way he had his entire life, slicked back and pomaded.

"Hello, Cal." His father greeted him with a wave while Brittney struggled to keep up with his longer strides. "The house looks great. I didn't know Dad wanted it redone or I would have gotten a crew over here."

Clint had retired from baseball after a storied career as a pitcher was ended by injury. He liked to say if they had ligament replacement procedures—Tommy John surgery—in his day, he would have come back better than ever, but Cal had doubts about that. Clint had been spoiled by his success, his hubris growing in conjunction with his contracts, money that Cal's mother had invested shrewdly. Clint had made a considerable sum in his career, but his first wife had quietly doubled it to ensure they could live comfortably for the rest of their lives. Clint enjoyed spending as much as he liked and being the center of attention, and once his own career ended he focused on his sons' athletic talents, and began using the new "windfall" to build an extravagant house that no one else in the family had wanted. Clint still didn't understand why none of his sons had been excited about a swim-up bar in the indoor swimming pool, but as long as his progeny made headlines as baseball players, Clint didn't complain.

By the time Clint cheated with Brittney, Cal's mother had seemed relieved to move back to the old house, to reclaim her previous life. Cal and his brothers had weathered their father's overblown pride and insistent pushing the only way they could—by excelling in the sport their father loved.

These days, however, Cal didn't feel the need to humor someone he found it tough to respect.

"Gramp never said he wanted the house painted," Cal clarified, emptying the remainder of the five-gallon bucket into his tray. "But it was obvious to me a lot of things needed repair and updating. I'm surprised you didn't notice."

Clint scrambled back a step to avoid getting paint on his expensive-looking loafers while Brittney craned her neck to stare into the garden next door where Josie was staking a row of sunflowers. The three dogs lay in shady patches around the garden's perimeter, never too far from her.

"Who's that?" Brittney asked, fluffing her red-gold curls, her nose wrinkling as she studied Josie.

Maybe the thought of manual labor was too much for her.

"Mom's caretaker," Cal explained, wondering if it was too rude to climb the ladder and keep working.

"Your mother has a caretaker now?" His father sounded impressed. Or was that envy in his voice?

Clint swiveled to see for himself.

"I'd better get back to work." Cal picked up the tray, balancing it carefully so the paint didn't slosh out.

"Wait, Son." Dad clapped him on the shoulder, jostling him enough to jar his arm and lose some of the bright white paint in the grass. "Sorry about that, but I wanted to talk to you about something."

"I've got a lot on my plate this afternoon—"

"This will only take a second," Clint insisted. "I made a call to one of my manager friends—you remember Dusty Reed—who's getting back in the business. I mentioned you, and you know how much Dusty thinks of you."

The news was actually more interesting than Cal had imagined. He set down the tray in the grass while Brittney wound a possessive hand around Clint's elbow.

"Is one of the teams interested in him?" Cal had played for Dusty briefly when he'd been in the minors. He liked the way Dusty coached, and the guy in turn seemed to appreciate what Cal brought to a team. Dusty had led a club deep in the playoffs his second year in the majors, and he'd been viewed as a big part of that run.

But he'd left coaching suddenly because of family problems three years ago. His son had been born with a heart defect and he'd set everything aside to focus on his family. Yet another reason Cal thought a lot of him.

"More than one," his father assured him. "You know his record. Teams are ready to look at a guy like that if they aren't getting off to a good start. He's spoken to three organizations."

"Three?" Cal knew his father liked to exaggerate things and he didn't want to get his hopes up.

But a coaching change could mean a roster change, especially if a team was struggling to begin with. And if the new coach was someone who thought well of Cal...there was a sliver of a chance his season could still turn around.

"Didn't he say three?" Clint looked to his wife for confirmation.

Brittney moved her cheeks in a way that might have been an attempt at a smile. A very, very small one.

"I don't remember, honey, and I really don't want to be

late for that party." She shifted from one foot to the other, her eyes still darting over to where Josie worked in the garden.

Because she was that interested in what went on at Clint's ex's home? Or was she that watchful of young women around her wealthy husband of the wandering eye?

"Don't let me keep you." Cal had no use for the vapid trophy wife who'd turned his father's head, and he'd never made a secret of it.

"I'll see if I can pull some strings, Son," Clint assured Cal. "We'll get you back in the game."

Cal knew if his brothers were here, they could defuse the tension with an eye roll or a joke, but it got on Cal's every last nerve that their father wanted to claim credit for careers they'd worked their asses off to build.

"No, Dad. *We* won't," he told him levelly. "Either there will be a need for me in the league this season, or there won't be, but my future depends on me."

His father frowned, and looked ready to argue, but Cal didn't care to hear it, so he continued, "But if you want credit for working on a project, why don't you come by tomorrow and help me finish painting Gramp's house?"

Brittney sighed loudly. "Of course he's not grateful, Clint. I told you he wouldn't be."

His father looked so disappointed for a moment, Cal half wished he could have reined it in. But then, Clint slid his arm around Brittney's waist and walked away from the farm.

Refusing to ruminate about his father Cal retrieved his

supplies and climbed the ladder to finish his painting for the day. His relationship with his father had always been tense, not because he tried to be his own advocate, but because he'd always tried to champion his younger brothers. Even back in the days when he'd looked up to his dad, he'd been well aware that Clint was a harsh critic of his kids.

Cal didn't care about the criticism for himself. Much.

But it ticked him off for his brothers' sake, who deserved better. When he got to the top of the ladder and settled into his rolling routine, he found himself scanning the garden for Josie.

A very welcome distraction from his visitor.

There was no sign of her outdoors anymore, though. Even the dogs were gone from the yard.

And damned if her absence didn't make the day slide from frustrating to downright dismal. He'd been avoiding her because he thought that's what she wanted, but now, realizing how much he missed her company, he wondered if there wasn't another way around those prickly defenses of hers.

IT WAS ALL Cal's fault, Josie told herself the next day as she carried a peach pie over to Everett Ramsey's house.

She had a taste for dessert now after Cal had brought her the decadent offerings from Char-Pie last week, and she seemed to crave pie night and day.

At least, she hoped it was coconut cream she was craving and not the studly baseball player himself. Either way, since she would only allow herself to satisfy one of those cravings, she had used the pantry staples Cal had stocked the kitchen with and baked her own peach pie. The peaches in Last Stand were supposed to be some of the best in Texas, and based on the fresh ones she'd eaten, she could see why.

The result of her baking smelled amazing and looked reasonably good, although she didn't have much experience in the pie-making department.

By afternoon, she'd decided to take it over to Everett's house. She wanted to talk to him about the bees she'd delivered to the watermelon fields, maybe see if there was any other help he would need on the farm once her caretaker work was done. Besides, this way, she wouldn't have to eat a whole pie on her own, and she could check on Everett with her own eyes since she hadn't seen him out with his walker in the last few days. While she hoped that Cal was keeping track of his grandfather, she couldn't be totally sure how dialed in he was to Everett's health since Cal seemed to be spending all his time working on the house next door.

He'd been painting walls, sanding porch rails, patching broken steps and weed whacking. Whatever he did, he seemed to do it either shirtless or sweaty enough to make his shirt cling to those highly memorable shoulders. She'd accidentally hoed up perfectly good bean plants multiple times because she'd been too busy taking surreptitious glances at his fine male physique.

Juggling the still-warm pie into one hand so she could knock on the front door, it opened before her knuckles met the hardwood.

Cal filled the doorframe with the broad chest she'd been thinking about just moments ago. He had a gray T-shirt on this time, which was probably just as well given how distracting he could be without it. A leather tool belt hung low on his hips over a pair of faded jeans.

"Oh." She lowered her hand, nearly forgetting why she'd come over in the first place. "Hi."

He leaned into the doorframe, blocking her path, but apparently not in a hurry to move, either.

"Is this your way of apologizing for not feeding me the other night?" he asked, in a voice that had circled around her dreams the past few nights.

"Um." She got a bit lost in his eyes. They were greener than she remembered from the last time she'd seen him up close. But he probably wasn't asking her about his eyes. "What was that again?"

"The pie." He pointed to the dish in her hands. "Is this a peace offering over the way you dismissed all attempts at a shared meal?"

Belatedly, she remembered the way they'd parted. With her convinced he was playing games.

"Charming men are a bit of a hot button for me right now," she admitted, shifting her feet on the welcome mat. "And technically the pie was for Everett."

"I'll be as uncharming as possible then." Cal straightened, reaching for the warm pie plate. "And since Everett's not here, I'll just leave this in the kitchen for him."

She kept her hold on it. "It's for Everett and me to *share*," she clarified, trying to peer past him into the darkened interior. "I wanted to check on him."

"My father picked him up an hour ago to take Gramp to see another neurology specialist in Houston." He studied her for a moment, his eyes narrowing. "I'll trade you a slice for an update on him."

Her gaze snagged on a ceiling fan perched precariously on a ladder in the middle of the living room, wires spilling out from the ceiling.

"Looks like you could use a hand in here more than you need a slice of pie." She refocused on Cal and realized there was a voltmeter stuffed in the breast pocket of his tee.

It was amazing the details she could overlook when pheromones attacked. If Tom Belvedere had looked like this man, she would have signed over more than her life savings. She probably would have thrown in her soul, to boot.

"I've got the project in hand," he assured her. "And you're making me lose the last bit of air conditioning by standing in the doorway."

"Only because you haven't invited me in." She was curious what he was doing. And she wanted to hear about Everett. Maybe she wanted to make amends with Cal too, in case she had overreacted the other night. "I've decided to take your trade after all. A slice for us both while you give me an update."

Cal stepped aside and waved her in. "In that case, welcome to the original Virgil Ramsey homestead, pride of Rough Hollow since 1856." He closed the front door behind her. "But I'll warn you, it's hot in here while I've got the main power shut off."

The air was still inside the home, but she guessed it wasn't as hot as some places might be in heat like this. The thick stone walls must do a good job of insulating. Wide-planked hardwood floors and high ceilings with exposed wooden rafters looked original to the house, as did the stone fireplace and hearth. There was detailed scrollwork on the wooden banister leading upstairs, the dark wainscoting giving the home an elegant and prosperous air.

"This is beautiful," she remarked as she edged past the ladder with the sideways ceiling fan. She followed Cal through the living area into the kitchen that had clearly been remodeled. The hardwood floors remained, and the painted cabinets appeared original, but the gray quartz countertops looked new, along with the pendant lamps over a breakfast bar.

"My grandmother loved this house," Cal told her, pulling open a drawer in the island and retrieving a pie lift. "She remodeled the kitchen a few years before she died."

Josie set the pie on the bar, admiring the view out the kitchen windows.

"It's nice how she blended the old and the new." Josie ran a hand over a barely visible seam in the countertop, recalling jobs she'd hired out at the apartment complex where so-called contractors botched the most basic counter installations. It didn't help that her mother's budget to fix anything always ranged between minuscule and nonexistent. "I'll bet she'd be glad to see all the work you're doing around here this week. You did a great job painting."

"Thanks." He took down two plates from the open shelving on the far wall. "It feels good to contribute something to the upkeep of the place. An unforeseen bright spot in an otherwise crappy spring."

She assumed he meant because of baseball and being released from his team, but she didn't ask since she clung to the hope that if she didn't pry further into his life, he wouldn't dig into hers. Instead, she focused on cutting two slices of pie.

"What does Everett think of the new paint job?" She carefully balanced the first piece on the lift and then settled it on the white stoneware plate.

Cal set two forks on the counter before sliding into one of the gray leather barstools. His elbow brushed her forearm and she redoubled her efforts to focus on the scent of peaches and not the appeal of clean male sweat.

"He's seemed sort of down the last few days. I can't tell if it's because he's not feeling well or..." He shrugged. "I don't know. Worried about something."

She wished his grandfather had been home so she could have spoken to him directly, possibly seen some other hint of what was bothering him. And, selfishly, she really had wanted to see if his farming operation needed any extra help later in the summer.

Now she watched Cal as he lifted the first bite to his mouth, crossing her fingers the pie was edible.

"Well?" The suspense was killing her, so she forked up a bite of her own.

The peaches were amazing, though the crust seemed a little off. Too stiff or something. Not flakey enough.

Cal frowned. "I can't decide if I should be honest or uncharming."

She felt disappointed. "I'm not going to put Char-Pie out of business, am I? You can be honest."

"Seriously? It's fantastic. And Everett's going to love it." He took another big bite.

And, really, was there any better endorsement than that? She couldn't deny a rush of pride in doing something well. For all that she was pleased with the progress of Hailey's garden, and that the bees seemed to be thriving in her care, those rewards weren't quite as fulfilling having someone tell her she'd done a good job. She'd grown accustomed to being harangued by her mother, who was never satisfied with a task unless Josie had managed to accomplish it without spending a cent. Cal's heartfelt praise was...nice.

They finished off their slices at the kitchen counter and caught up on news. She told him about the bee transfer to the watermelon fields, and he explained why the ceiling fan job was tricky. She even talked him into letting her help with replacing it since she knew far more about installing fixtures than he would ever guess.

Besides, she wasn't offering to lend a hand just so she had an excuse to linger here with him, although she couldn't deny she'd missed seeing him. She still nursed a hope that if Everett saw she worked hard and was capable, he might offer her some kind of seasonal employment that could get her on her feet again.

Following Cal into the living area, she listened to his explanation about wiring the ceiling fan to work with the switches. He'd made a careful diagram for himself with notes about what colors connected where in order to make the light and fan options work with the switch.

"The trouble is, the old mounting system doesn't have the brackets to balance the fan." He pointed to the original woodwork around the old fixture, which he clearly hadn't wanted to ruin. "In other words, I'm stuck trying to hold it high enough to wire it and still having enough hands to connect everything."

"So I'll hold it and you wire."

"It's heavy though," he eyed her dubiously. "And it might take me a few minutes, so you'd have to hold it for a while."

"If we take the fan blades back off, it'll be lighter," she suggested, taking in the fully assembled unit on the ladder. "Removing the light kit would help too, and it's probably easy to put together once you have it up there."

She knew for a fact that it was, since she'd made the same rookie mistakes installing ceiling fans for Mrs. Wolenski, one of her favorite tenants who baked cookies every week to share with neighbors. But she hated to be too specific about her experience since the last thing she needed was Cal poking around her past.

If there were charges against her in Florida for doing contracting work without a license, she didn't need anyone in Last Stand to know about it. It wasn't some federal offense that would get her dragged back to her home state. But it would be endlessly humiliating. She'd debated calling the code enforcement officer back home and asking about it, but would that only draw attention to her mother's building? Stir trouble where maybe there was none? She knew it was wrong to just bury her head in the sand, but she wasn't ready to make those phone calls yet when she felt like she was finally shaking off some of the frustrations of her past.

"It will be a piece of cake to do it that way." Cal grinned at her, dazzling her a little with the magnitude of his smile. His very masculine appeal. "Good thinking."

She watched as he used a cordless drill to remove the extra hardware, stripping down the unit to something more manageable for her to hold. Once he was absorbed in the task, she sneaked a peek at his wiring diagram to be sure it made sense since he'd admitted he'd had trouble making all the functions work from the switches. While she was still comparing his notes to the directions that came with the unit, Cal grabbed an extra stool from the kitchen for him to stand on so they could work side by side.

"Are you ready?" he asked once he had everything prepped. "I can carry it up there so you don't have to juggle the base while you're on the ladder."

"I'm ready." She approved of his wiring diagram, and she noticed he carefully taped it on the ceiling for easy reference. "You're sure the power is off?"

He'd told her that's why the air conditioning wasn't on, but she flipped a switch just to double-check.

"Positive. I want to get this finished up before Everett gets home so the place can start cooling down." Cal stepped onto the stool while she climbed the ladder.

Once they were both in place, he passed over the ceiling fan base.

"You're sure you'll be okay?" he asked, before giving her the full weight of it.

A shiver of awareness passed through her at the brush of his hands on hers. The concern in his green eyes made her belly flip.

"I'll be fine."

She cradled the unit against her while he connected wires and screwed on wire nuts. It was a chance to watch him up close and unobserved, and she let her gaze roam from the muscles in his arms to his broad shoulders and chest. She was close enough to breath in the scent of his soap, to see the sheen on his skin from the heat of the day.

"There," he announced. "It's all wired. Now I just need to fasten it up there." His gaze slid over to hers, where he may have caught her ogling him.

She snapped her attention back to his eyes. "You don't want to flip the power on to make sure it all works first?"

His gaze never wavered.

"Everything works," he assured her, the air between them heating up. "We just need to fit things together."

His hands covered hers in a touch that stole her breath away. But then, he pushed gently, helping her raise the unit fully to the ceiling so he could screw the new base into place.

She didn't let go because she didn't want to impede the project, but her palms were effectively trapped under his for a long moment while he aligned everything. How could she have ever guessed that feeling the points of pressure gently shifting on the back of her hand would feel so intimate?

"If I let go to grab the drill, will you be okay?" he asked, their arms still raised over their heads.

She nodded, not trusting herself to speak.

When he let go of her, he moved quickly to retrieve the cordless drill from the tool belt. Once he had two of the screws in place, she let go while he made quick work of the last four.

After he finished, she watched him lean back to admire their handiwork. She started to back down the ladder carefully. Cal stepped off the stool.

His feet hit the floor faster than hers, giving him enough time to steady the ladder for her before she reached the last rung. With his arms bracketing her body, she was highly aware of him. Her right hip grazed his midsection, a brush of denim against cotton. Heat against longing.

She rocked back on her heels as she landed on the hardwood, very close to him. Visions of landing in his arms, feeling him wrapped around her, made her heart gallop.

"Thanks, Josie." He only lingered for a moment before stepping away, giving her space. "You saved me a lot of time."

It took her a moment to remember what he was talking about since her thoughts were heated in the extreme. She resisted the urge to tug her shirt away from her skin and billow the fabric like a fan to cool down.

Fan. She remembered that's how she'd saved him a lot of time.

"No problem." She stretched her lips in a forced smile, recognizing she'd hit her personal limit of how much Cal she could indulge in at one time without crossing a line she would only regret. She needed to leave before she did something foolish, like plaster herself against him for a better feel. "I'll let you finish up."

It would be too revealing if she sprinted for the exit, so she forced herself to turn toward the door slowly. Normally. As if she was just a friend taking her leave and not a woman fighting a crush on a hot guy.

"I'd like to thank you."

His words slowed her step.

"That's not necessary." A few days away from Cal had made her forget how potent the attraction was. Or maybe a few days away had strengthened it because she felt like a giant rubber band was hauling her back toward him. "I'm happy to lend a hand. Tell Everett I was sorry to miss him."

"You don't want to hear my offer?" The deep rumble of

his voice traveled along her skin in the too-still room. "I would like to take you to a ball game tomorrow. See my kid brother play."

Surprised, she felt a tug of curiosity about his family. She'd wanted to learn more about him, and suddenly, he seemed to be opening that door. But she couldn't appease her curiosity about Cal when she was supposed to be wary around him.

"You've done too much for me already." She wasn't used to taking help from anyone and she found the terrain tricky to navigate, especially with all of the other dynamics between her and Cal. "If you hadn't gotten the groceries, I would have never been able to make the pie."

"And you repaid me with pie," he reminded her, following her toward the door.

She wanted to argue, but he didn't give her a chance. Instead, he kept talking.

"Besides, you'd be doing me a favor at the same time."

"So your thank-you to me does double duty as a favor to you?" She folded her arms, eyeing him skeptically.

Amused in spite of herself.

"I have the feeling my dad will show up at the game with his wife and…" The stony expression that stole across his face told her more than any words. "I could use a buffer."

"I'd be your buffer," she clarified, drawn to him and his complicated life that he wasn't prepared to share.

She couldn't help but identify with that.

"Okay, when you put it like that, I sound like a selfish

ass, but I genuinely thought you might enjoy a night out since you're tied to the house without a vehicle. It's not like I'm angling for dinner or anything with Casanova expectations." He obviously hadn't forgotten her accusations when he'd invited her to share a meal with him the last time. "It's just a game."

The idea tempted her. Because as much as she appreciated the remoteness of Hailey Decker's home to recover from all that life had thrown at her, she had been lonely sometimes. She'd had fun the day she spent at Rough Hollow Farm with Cal. Besides, she still nurtured hopes of extending her stay in Last Stand long enough to earn some more money to start over. Fostering a relationship with Cal's prominent family would probably be a good idea.

"Just a game?" she mused aloud, thinking it over. "I have the feeling the Ramseys take baseball more seriously than that."

"You'll never know if you're not in the stands with me tomorrow night." He shrugged like it was no big deal. "Did I mention baseball happens to be the great American pastime?"

He was entirely too charming. And even when she saw it a mile away, she couldn't resist the chance for an outing. An opportunity to learn more about him.

"In that case, I accept your invitation." She hoped she wouldn't regret it.

But she'd be lying if she said she wasn't looking forward to a night out with Cal.

Chapter Six

"SO YOUR BROTHER plays in Triple-A?" Josie asked from the passenger seat of his convertible.

The trip to the ballpark was over an hour's drive, and the conversation on the way into San Antonio had been pleasant. She'd talked to him about the things she enjoyed around the farmhouse and shared some anecdotes about his mom's dogs. He'd filled her in on his dad's refusal to work Everett's farm, and the pressure he'd applied to his sons to chase the baseball dream. Cal had figured he needed to bring her up to speed a bit on that dynamic given that Clint Ramsey would make himself plenty visible around the ballpark tonight.

His grip tightened on the steering wheel. Better to focus on the question she'd asked him. Especially since he wanted her to have a good time tonight.

"Both of my brothers are in Triple-A." He glanced over at her while she snapped a photo out the passenger window. "Although Nate has been back and forth between Double-A and Triple-A a good bit over the last two seasons. Tonight we'll see Nate's team."

Josie set her phone back in her lap and he wondered what she'd seen that had been photo-worthy. It looked like dry fields on either side of the road to him.

"Nate's the next oldest?" She pulled off her sunglasses and tucked them in the sack she used like a handbag.

She'd worn a denim skirt and a purple T-shirt with the cover art for a Jane Austen novel on it. He'd noticed that any time she took a break from work, she had a book in her hands. Her hair was in a braid again, something he guessed was her nod to the heat. A few pieces curled around her face.

"Yes. He's a year and a half younger than me, and Wes is three years younger than I am." They'd been close growing up, but once they'd started playing ball professionally, it had been next to impossible to see each other during the season.

A problem Cal didn't have anymore now that he had nowhere to report. The knowledge still ate at him.

"And you think your father will be at the game too?"

"I know he will." The old man couldn't stay away from baseball. Cal knew that losing his spot on a major league roster this year was killing his father. "Whenever Wes or Nate have had games in the vicinity, Dad will hire a big van to take friends to the ballpark for the night. What seats he doesn't fill with friends, he'll offer to local bars to give away as happy-hour prizes."

"That seems supportive." She picked at a frayed piece of the unhemmed denim skirt.

"Yes and no." Cal remembered plenty of his own games where his father had been in the crowd. "My dad mostly enjoys basking in his own glory, but if Nate has a good game, he'll be glad to have some friends and family around afterward."

"What if he doesn't have a good game?" She retrieved her phone to take another photo out her window, and this time, Cal could see she was lining up a shot of a farm stand advertising pick-your-own peaches.

"Then Nate will have to decide if it's worth dealing with the old man's breakdown of everything he did wrong before he can enjoy the pleasure of anyone else's company." Cal steered into the passing lane as traffic started picking up.

"Really?" She sounded surprised. "I can't picture your mother married to someone like that. She's so mellow."

"She might be making up for all the years she dealt with him." He hadn't considered that before. Another reminder of how focused he'd been on his career. "She never used to do things like mission trips or beekeeping when they were together."

"Then good for her. She seems happy."

"She deserves to be," he said a little more fiercely than he'd intended. "I could forgive my father for how he treats me, but I can't overlook how he disrespected my mom. For that matter, it ticks me off how little he does for Everett."

"That's where your buffer comes in, right?" Josie shifted in her seat, crossing her legs in the opposite direction in a move that pulled his attention from the road for a split second. "Any tips for how I should do my job tonight?"

He refocused his eyes on the road, but memories of her curves filled his head anyway. He flipped on his blinker to move to the right lane for their next exit.

"Just having you next to me will keep me from feeling any need to talk to him. No need to do anything special." And, really, he hadn't been totally honest with her about his motives for wanting her at the game. Because while having her there would give him distance from his dad, what he needed from her even more was the sexy distraction she would provide as he sat through the first game he had to watch now that he wasn't a player any longer.

She was silent for a long moment. When he looked her way, she was biting her lip, tension obvious in the downward angle of her brows.

"You think I'm a first-class spoiled brat for not wanting to talk to my own father, don't you?" He hadn't meant to come off like an entitled jock who thought the world revolved around him.

"Far from it." Her voice sounded faraway. Thoughtful. "I was just thinking how useful it would be to have a buffer around my own difficult parent."

He wanted to ask more about that—to find out which one of her parents she viewed as challenging, but his phone buzzed through the car's stereo sound system, the dashboard screen alerting him that his brother was on the line.

"Do you mind if I take this?" he asked, his finger hovering near the connect button.

"Go right ahead." She flipped her own phone over to amuse herself, or maybe just to give him the illusion of privacy.

Tapping the screen, he picked up the call.

"I'm five minutes from the stadium, Bro. You ready for game time?" Cal hadn't spoken to Nate in weeks. But then, his brothers would understand better than anyone how being released from his team would mess with his mind.

No doubt, they'd simply been giving him space to deal with it on his own terms.

"Depends. If 'bottom of the order' equals ready, then I guess I'm good to go," Nate announced, his voice revealing none of the angst that must have come with the news.

"Of all the nights for the bench boss to move you around in the order, it has to be tonight?" Cal shook his head, disgusted on Nate's behalf.

The manager of his brother's club—Moose Byers—had been a long-ago rival of their father's, and the guy had been bitter his whole life that he hadn't managed to make a career as a player while Clint had. Cal guessed that even the most charming of the Ramsey men—Nate by a long shot— wouldn't have dissuaded Moose from his old grudge.

"What are the odds Dad will be more pissed at Moose than me when he gets the news?" Nate's voice came through the stereo speakers tinny and echoing, and Cal guessed he was somewhere in the locker room.

"With Dad there's no shortage of blame to spread around. I'm guessing there's an equal amount of anger for both of you."

"Clint Ramsey, ever the diplomat," Nate said wryly, although there was a hint of humor behind it.

Of the three brothers, Nate had possessed the best ability

to shake off a bad mood. He was the most laid-back, the most fun to be around.

"If I don't see you in the stands after—" Cal began, wanting to make a plan for a post-game visit if Nate preferred to avoid their father.

He steered the vehicle through a knot of traffic near the stadium entrance, choosing a lane moving faster.

"I'll be there either way," Nate assured him, a P.A. system sounding in the background on his end of the call.

"Yeah?" He wouldn't press his brother about it, but Cal found it tough to believe Nate would put in an appearance if he had a rough night at the plate.

"For sure." There were some scuffling noises on Nate's end. "Rumor has it Keely Harper is making the trip to see the game."

Cal remembered Nate's on-again, off-again girlfriend from high school. She'd cut and run as soon as Nate got drafted, apparently not interested in sticking with him through the lean years of the minor leagues, when paychecks weren't even minimum wage.

He must have been silent a beat too long since Josie peered over at him, one eyebrow raised. But before he could craft a nonjudgmental reply, Nate spoke again.

"I've got to get out on the field, Cal. See you soon." The call disconnected as Cal pulled into a parking spot outside the stadium.

While he struggled to figure out why Nate would want to see a woman who'd walked away during the hard times,

Cal switched off the engine and refocused his attention on his date for the game.

"Ready?" His curt tone made him realize how much his brother's call had riled him.

Gauging by Josie's pursed lips, she hadn't missed the edge in his voice either. She studied him across the console while a young family dressed in team colors walked past the car.

"Depends. I'm ready for baseball. I'm not sure if I'm ready for family drama." Her hands were clenched tightly in her lap.

"With the Ramseys, the two go hand in hand." Yet another facet of his major league career that he would miss— the aura of success around a professional at that level gave him a way to distance himself from the messed-up sports psychology that ran through his family tree.

"What if I get midway through the game and discover I'm in over my head?" The seriousness in her voice caught him off guard. Made him realize how much he'd stressed her out with the talk of his family dynamics.

Regret circled through him. He hadn't meant to drag her into the chest-thumping toxicity that always seemed to simmer around his dad. He forced himself to breathe out his own frustrations so he could reassure her.

"We make our way to the exit and don't look back." He could always catch up with Nate on the road. "It's more important to me that you have a good time."

She nodded, but her expression remained skeptical. Her

pretty eyes darted around uneasily.

He took one of her hands in his and gently squeezed.

"It is America's pastime," he reminded her. "Most people think it's fun."

Her gaze dropped to where he touched her. He could feel her pulse hammer wildly at the base of her thumb. Wishing he could soothe her worries, he stroked a knuckle over the throbbing vein.

Just then, with the scent of her fragrance tickling his nose and the softness of her skin calling to his hands, he wanted to taste her. What if he lowered his mouth to hers for a kiss right here? Right now?

"Fair warning, Cal. I'm not most people." She tugged her hand from his and levered open the passenger door before he could get around the car and help her out.

Cal scrambled to follow her while the music from the baseball stadium blared out onto the parking area over the sound system. The scent of popcorn and hot dogs already permeated the air, as a couple of boys in ball caps streaked past playing a game of tag.

Tonight, he needed Josie. And damned if he didn't want her, too. She might be hiding secrets of her own, but at least he understood that about her from the start. This way, there wouldn't be any surprises or false promises. No blame or broken hearts when it ended.

From where he was standing, it looked like the start of a promising temporary relationship.

All he had to do was convince her of that.

IT TOOK JOSIE three innings before she could focus on the game.

The stadium was only half-full, but that still put her in a crowd of over three thousand people with all the noise and activity that went with it. For someone more comfortable at home reading a good book, the venue was a little overwhelming. The vendors carrying peanuts and cotton candy through the hard metal stands shouted prices, while a commentator made observations about the game over a loudspeaker system. Fans waved foam fingers and felt pennant flags. As the sun set over perfectly mown grass, the stadium lights came on, illuminating the field.

But the action on the field was only a small part of what claimed her attention. More near at hand, the Ramsey family drama played out in living color. Clint Ramsey was obviously a popular guy, and he'd arrived after the rest of his "party bus" guests had already been seated in a special luxury suite with tables and private service for their group. She and Cal had arrived on the open deck first to claim their seats during batting practice, but within an hour, the reserved section filled with visitors from Last Stand ready to support a hometown player.

Cal shook hands and made a point of introducing her to a handful of people. She spent some time visiting with a local doctor, Graham McBride, and his girlfriend Bella Benson who was a blonde beauty with rainbow stripes at the ends of her hair. Josie never settled into a conversation for long though, as Cal navigated them through the crowd. She guessed that having her there gave him something to talk about besides his own baseball career. Right about the time someone would say, "Sorry to hear—" Cal would jump in with: "Have you met Josie?"

She could tell how much everyone liked Cal by the way they all let the topic slide.

Right up until Cal's father had arrived midway through the second inning. She'd recognized him from photographs at Hailey's house. Clint Ramsey might be graying and a little less muscular than his offspring, but he was still a handsome man. He'd strolled onto the party deck with his carefully coiffed wife, greeting people on all sides, but never acknowledging his son.

"Are the two of you not on speaking terms?" she asked Cal softly once the third inning began and the two Ramsey men hadn't greeted one another.

She and Cal shared a round table closest to the field on the multi-level party deck just past the bleachers on the third base side. Cal's father and his wife were seated at a table behind them.

"We're speaking. This is normal." Cal sipped his beer before continuing. "How are you liking the game?"

"There's way too much for my brain to process. Honestly, I've hardly noticed the game." She peered up at the flashing screen in the outfield that posted player statistics, ads and goofy graphics between batters. "The massive television over there, for example. It's like an assault on the senses."

Cal laughed lightly, a sound she was coming to enjoy the longer she knew him. He didn't seem like a man who laughed often enough.

"What a refreshing perspective. Cheers to you for finding other things to focus on." He clinked his glass to her mostly full beer still on the table. "Before we were old enough to play baseball, my father would drag us to games and critique our stat books afterward. So even when we couldn't make our own stats, we were graded on how efficiently we recorded other people's."

"Stat books?" She had no idea what he was talking about.

"Doesn't matter." He set his beer back down. "Don't look now, but he's headed this way."

Tension pulled her muscles tight, making her wonder why she'd agree to come when her own relationship with a parent was so fraught with stress. As if she had a clue how to defuse that sort of situation. But then again, she'd found it tough to deny Cal help when he'd been willing to admit that weakness himself.

She ground her teeth together and willed herself to be pleasant. Social. Normal. But when she glanced around to greet Cal's father, she noticed he wasn't looking at her.

Dressed in a crisp white polo shirt and khakis, the elder Ramsey's attention was on the field even when he dropped into the open bench seat across from Cal.

"Of all the nights for Moose to drop Nate in the order it had to be tonight," the elder Ramsey began without preamble. "What are the chances your brother will get a hit when he's demoralized over batting ninth?"

Josie watched Cal's jaw flex. Felt the strain in the air. Maybe it was because her own mother treated her like a second-class citizen, but something in her wouldn't let Cal's father ruin her night at the ballpark with Cal.

"Hi," she greeted him brightly, extending her hand across the table. "I'm Josie Vance."

Slowly, Cal's father hauled his attention from the field to rest on her. His green eyes were familiar enough since Cal possessed the same shade of spring grass. But whereas Cal's smile was one hundred percent genuine, his father's seemed like an overused reflex and a little condescending besides.

"Nice to meet you, Josie Vance. I'm Clint Ramsey." He shook her hand, but he didn't seem terribly enthused about it.

Cal, on the other hand, relaxed a fraction beside her. She couldn't see it so much as feel it—the slightest decrease in friction. Which meant she was far too in tune to the man's every mood.

"You must be proud to see how many people turned out to cheer on your son." She waved an arm to indicate the nearly one hundred people filling the reserved section of the park.

Beyond the people who'd ridden the bus Clint had reserved, many residents of Last Stand had made the trip on their own, joining the group at the field. There were tables full of neighbors catching up on gossip, downing hot dogs, and admiring one another's kids. A few preschoolers pushed trucks around the planked floor, weaving in and out of tables and knees.

"Proud? Yes." Clint gave her a wink. "Although it's possible half of them are here for the free food."

"No one drives an hour for the sake of a hot dog," she assured him.

The crowd on the bleachers outside the party deck erupted in applause, drawing her attention from the conversation. Around her, a murmur of excited interest went through the Last Stand visitors, and she heard someone behind her say, "Nate's up next."

The light-up display board in left field didn't show photos of the visiting team's player like it did for the home team, but it did broadcast Nate Ramsey's name and number. She could feel the tension of the two men on either side of the table. Both Cal and Clint were focused on the field where the tall, rangy ballplayer seemed to take his time getting comfortable in the batter's box. He adjusted gloves, tapped his cleats with his bat, repositioned his feet, then tugged on his batting helmet in a ritual that looked borderline obsessive compulsive to her admittedly untrained eye.

No one around her seemed to think anything of it, however. For the first time, she saw the full extent of the resemblance between Cal and his father. They wore identical strained expressions, like the future of the free world rested on this at-bat.

"Let's go, Nate!" a man shouted behind her.

Josie jolted, looking over her shoulder just as a couple of women wolf-whistled then collapsed into laughter.

Biting her lip as she turned back to face the field, Josie found it all sorts of distracting. To make things worse, she'd failed to see the first pitch, but it must have happened because the scoreboard announced a gleeful "Strike One" in rainbow-colored letters, the words spiraling around the screen and flashing.

Clint swore. Cal leaned closer to the field. She forced herself to watch the pitcher more closely this time, and she spotted the ball when it left his glove, but she missed whatever Nate did on his end.

The "Strike Two" announcement was even more celebratory, with digital fireworks exploding in the background. Nate backed out of the box and walked in a circle, watching his coach give a sign before he returned to the batter's box. Repeated the helmet-tugging thing.

"You've got to get your bat off your shoulder in this situation, Josie," Clint imparted with a tone of helpfulness that struck her as somewhat demeaning.

"I'm sure your son is aware of that," she returned quietly, not bothering to look his way.

She thought she saw Cal's shoulders twitch, however, and hoped that meant she was functioning well in the buffer role. Too bad she couldn't bring him to Florida with her to run interference the next time she saw her mother. If she ever went back to Florida.

And wasn't that a foolish wish? She gave herself a little shake as she realized that she was letting herself like Cal too much.

When the next pitch came, the crack of the bat was audible proof he'd hit it, infusing her with a moment of hope before she realized he'd fouled it off somewhere behind him. He did that twice more.

The third time the bat connected, however, the ball sailed in a line drive to right field. The player out there had to run after it to throw it in, and his throw was garbage, apparently, as it bounced around the shortstop's feet. Around her, everyone on the deck was going wild, shouting and clapping for Nate.

Everyone except for his father and brother, oddly. Clint gave a nod of satisfaction, though. Cal clapped twice.

And how was that for bizarre family dynamics? She planned to quiz Cal about it on the way home from the game. In the end, Nate got to second and drove in a run, but the next batter struck out to end the half inning.

Clint shifted in his seat and stood to leave, then clapped Cal on the shoulder. "Looks like Nate staved off following in your footsteps for another night."

The comment was uttered so good-naturedly, with that ever-present smile, it took Josie a moment to understand what he meant as Clint stalked away. Cal didn't say anything, just turned back toward the table to take another sip of his beer. Even then, his neutral expression made her wonder if she'd misunderstood.

"Did he mean—" she began.

"That Nate's lucky he won't get cut from his team the way I got cut from mine?" Cal nodded. "Yes. That's exactly what he meant."

She'd thought her mother was needlessly cruel with the way she criticized Josie's work, her character, and her choices. But there was something troubling about a father who tried to undermine offspring who succeeded in a sport that was only a dream for most people.

"How petty." She wondered what it had been like for Cal and his brothers to grow up with that kind of pressure. For that matter, their father's know-it-all expertise about their jobs had to affect the relationships they had with him even as adults. Who wanted a parent second-guessing their every career move?

"He was probably still smarting from that hot dog comment," Cal teased, a wicked grin unfurling as he took her hand and squeezed it. "I wish I'd seen the look on his face when you told him no one would drive this far for a hot dog."

The contact of his fingers wrapped around her palm felt sweetly natural, right. At the same time, it felt dizzyingly intoxicating. Far more effective than her two sips of beer.

Logic told her she shouldn't like touching him so much when she knew she couldn't trust her instincts where men were concerned. But it was tough to make her body obey her brain's commands when Cal smiled at her that way. Like they shared a secret. Like they understood each other on some level.

"He's an unusual man," she said finally, taking his comment literally since she wasn't sure how else to respond. "I thought most fathers couldn't wait to take credit for their sons' successes, but he seems determined to not acknowledge yours."

"That's because all of life is a competition in the Clint Ramsey world, and he's determined to win. Not to mention, right now he considers me a failure." He squeezed her hand. "Now, let's forget about him for a little while so I can take you around the stadium and show you the behind-the-scenes world of a player."

Her heart rate sped faster at Cal's touch. The promise of being alone with him. She should say no, of course. She'd come here to be a buffer and take in a game.

But seeing this other side of Cal—a chink in the armor he showed the world as a professional athlete—made her want to know him better. Made her willing to risk spending more time with him. Alone.

She took a deep breath and blurted, "What are we waiting for?"

Chapter Seven

"CALVIN RAMSEY, IT'S good to see you remember your roots." Buck Wyman, the stadium's head of security, greeted Cal with a bear hug and a thump on the back that would have felled a smaller man. Built like an NFL lineman, Buck had held the head of security job during the year Cal played in the Texas league and he'd been a good friend to have. "Welcome home."

Buck stood at the top of the stairway that led to the underground locker rooms, clubhouse and team offices, places that Cal wanted to point out to Josie on a quick tour of the facility. Mostly, he'd needed a retreat from his father and the strain of watching his first professional ball game since getting cut from his team. He'd known it would be tough to get through the evening, but his father's running commentary on Nate's performance only made it worse. Cal knew it was his father's way of articulating his disappointment in Cal.

"Thank you." Cal eased back enough to draw Josie forward to make introductions. "I wanted to give Josie a quick tour before Nate comes up in the batting order again. Is that okay?"

"Are you kidding me? There are a lot of guys downstairs who will be damned thrilled to see you, Cal. It's not often we get visiting royalty." Buck stepped aside to let them pass. "Take your time. And thanks for that Atlanta Rebels bag you sent my daughter. She's the envy of her softball team."

"My pleasure," Cal assured him as he led Josie down the stairs, liking the feel of her hand in his.

He was surprised he'd talked her into the private tour, but then, he didn't think she had much use for crowds given the way she'd holed up in his mother's house for months straight. And her irritation with his father had been apparent. So maybe she'd only agreed to go with him to escape the busy party deck full of Last Stand residents.

Behind them, he could hear the fans cheer, letting him know the home team got a hit. There were no speakers in this part of the building, however, so he couldn't hear the game announcer.

"Visiting royalty?" Josie spoke softly as they passed the team's rehabilitation room where the bikes, weights and low trampoline all sat empty.

"That may have been overstating the case," Cal admitted, guiding her past the home team's clubhouse where the widescreen television still showed an eighties teen flick. The leather couches were grouped around it in the middle of the lockers, just the way he remembered from his year playing here. "But the guys in the organization have a lot of respect for anyone who makes it to the next level. They know better than most how few people get that call."

They were also too tactful to comment on Cal's untimely departure from his previous team, something he appreciated. Something his father would never understand.

"It must be nice to have a warm homecoming." Josie sounded wistful as she peered into the clubhouse operations room—a glorified name for the kitchen and laundry areas. "You certainly didn't receive much of a welcome in Last Stand between Everett's injuries and your mom's absence."

She still hadn't slid her hand free. He couldn't remember the last time he'd held hands with a woman. Let alone when it had affected him this way. He wanted to strategize ways to keep touching her. Ways to touch her even more.

"I don't mind keeping a low profile." He didn't see the operations manager, so he kept moving through the building, pointing out some of the offices while memories bombarded him from the year he'd played in this league.

So many damn memories. The time on the field was only a small portion of a player's life. Just as many hours unfolded in rooms like these—space shared with teammates at home and on the road. The major league level had upgraded team facilities, better meals, better hotel rooms. But the game was no different. If anything, the fatter paychecks of the top-tier players took away a lot of the camaraderie built in the minors. Players went their own ways, buying big mansions far from the stadium, bringing families on the road with them.

He'd seen it happen in his time in Atlanta, the bonds of brotherhood eroding. Even so, he'd miss being part of a team. Baseball had been a huge facet of his life up until four weeks ago. Josie halted in the echoing hallway beside him, tugging him to a stop.

"Should we have invited Everett to the game with us?" she asked, pausing in front of a row of drink machines.

They'd reached the end of the home team's facilities, and he didn't know the security guard who sat near the visiting team's locker area just up ahead. Cal pivoted to return the way they'd come.

"Everett has never been a baseball fan." Understatement of the year. He'd tried to explain to her some of the family dynamics in the car on the way to the game, but he must not have clarified that part. "Gramp never forgave Dad for turning his back on Rough Hollow. That land has been in the Ramsey family for generations, first as a ranch and then as a farm and orchards."

It seemed unfair to Everett that Clint had never let his kids seriously consider working the land, molding his sons' baseball careers from the time they were old enough to throw a ball, and alienating his only daughter in a way that ensured she didn't feel the same ties to the family or land. For Cal's part, he was already signing a contract with a team by the time he'd reached the age to make his own decisions. It wasn't easy to walk away from the only job he'd trained for, and he knew his brothers had been in the same boat.

Although, now that Cal had lost his spot, he needed to give the future—and the land—more thought.

Josie followed more slowly, the sounds of the game still

audible on the P.A. system speakers inside the rooms they passed. Cal noticed the wives' and family lounge was empty, so he guided Josie in there. The space wasn't much bigger than an average living room, but there was a closed-circuit feed of the game from a camera behind home plate along with a couple of well-used leather couches. "Even so, I'm surprised Everett wouldn't want to cheer on Nate," Josie observed as she let go of his hand and took a seat beside him on the couch. Her knees fell toward his, close but not touching. "I know he's proud of you. And your brothers, too."

Cal guessed Gramp would be more proud if one of the grandsons stepped up to take over the management of the farming operation, but he didn't want to dwell on family drama. Just being back in a ballpark for the first time— without a uniform—was tough enough for him tonight.

"I'm just glad I convinced you to be here," he told her honestly. "Thanks for making the trip with me."

Seated on the edge of the couch cushion, she peered into a wicker basket full of toys on a scarred wooden coffee table, then pulled out a yellow plastic truck. "As much as I love the farmhouse, I will admit that it's been fun having some outings since you showed up in Last Stand."

She dug deeper in the basket and found a green plastic trailer meant to hitch to the truck, then attached the two of them together.

"How much longer will you be in town?" he asked carefully, remembering how skittish she'd been about personal questions.

But he'd shared a whole lot about himself today. Surely it wasn't too much to ask that she reciprocate in small measure. Still, he wondered if her sudden fascination with the toys in the family lounge was a sign of nervousness.

"Your mother returns from her trip in two weeks."

"Two weeks." It didn't sound like enough time for how well he'd like to get to know Josie.

Then again, maybe it was the perfect time frame for two people in transition. Two people who didn't know what next month held.

"The last time I invited you to have dinner with me, you interpreted it as a come-on line," he began, not wanting to make the same mistake with her again.

"Because it was." She set down the truck and the trailer and met his gaze, giving him her full attention. "And I can't afford to play games."

He appreciated her candor. He sat forward on the couch to get closer to her, his thigh grazing her knee as he shifted.

"Okay. That's fair," he acknowledged, his pulse kicking faster as her blue eyes roamed over him briefly. "I understand why. But what if we were careful to limit our expectations? We might really enjoy the next two weeks more...together."

She arched a dark eyebrow at him. "Calvin Ramsey, are you suggesting a two-week affair?"

"I'm strongly advising it." He had thought about this, and based on the way she'd dodged his last round of efforts to flirt with her, he figured being straightforward would be the best approach.

"For two weeks?" Her gaze narrowed as she studied him. "That sounds perilously close to playing games."

"I'm one hundred percent serious about this." He took her hand in his and met her gaze. Just that simple touch felt so damn good, he found himself bringing her palm to his lips. Pressing a lingering kiss there. "Josie, the last time I flirted with you for fun, you avoided me for two days afterward, so I'm not going to make that mistake again. I want to be direct about what I want."

She swallowed hard, her gaze lingering on the place where he'd kissed her.

"Did I mention I'm recovering from some unhappy romantic issues?" She blinked up at him while, on the screen behind her, another inning came to an end.

He was more than ready for the game to finish so he could take her home and show her how good they could be together. He only needed to see Nate afterward and they could leave.

"Maybe an affair will help you put that in the past. Allow you to move on." He reached to brush back a dark curl that had escaped her braid, skimming along the creamy skin of her cheek to tuck the hair behind her ear.

And yes, maybe he wanted to see the pulse leap at the base of her throat. To feel the hitch in her breath against his palm.

"That seems like thin rationalization for intimacy." Her voice was a rasp of air.

Her eyes very aware of him.

"I've got a better one," he assured her, canting closer.

Never taking his gaze from hers so he could see any hesitation. Any hint of uncertainty.

"I'm listening." The blue vein at the base of her neck throbbed faster. Or maybe he just felt the rapid-fire beat at her wrist where he still held her hand.

"You don't need to listen." He cupped her chin. Skimmed his thumb along the fullness of her lower lip. "Just feel."

When his mouth replaced his thumb, he felt her gasp, the tiny intake of breath drawing him in. His eyes closed then, all the better to taste her. Her lips were so soft against his. She tasted like cinnamon.

Cal let go of her hand to slide his palm around her back, steadying her. Her fingers landed on his shoulder, a featherlight touch that left him burning for more. But he wanted— no, needed—to go slow. He'd come this far. Now that he knew what it might be like between them, there was no way he was going to risk pushing too fast.

With more than a little regret, he broke off the kiss, but didn't edge away. He stayed right there, tipping his forehead to hers until he found the strength to ease back.

It gratified the hell out of him to see Josie run the tip of her tongue over her lip. A quick, surreptitious taste that sent a surge of longing through him so strong it stole his breath.

"I'll grant you this," she said finally, her voice light but certain. "That was a whole lot more persuasive than your first reason."

"I've been wanting to do that since the first night in my mother's kitchen," he admitted, scavenging the will to straighten, knowing he'd never see the end of the game if he kept touching her this way. "And now that you know what I want, the next move is yours."

JOSIE COULDN'T THINK about anything else but that kiss through the game's final innings. What did she want to happen next? She wanted more time with Cal. Of course she did. He was an incredibly appealing man. Add to that his obvious closeness with his family—doing chores for Everett, showing up here tonight for Nate even though it clearly made him uncomfortable on a lot of levels—and Josie was sorely tempted to accept his invitation for an affair.

It sounded so illicit. So hot. Even the time limit held appeal for her since she was skittish of men after the Tom Belvedere disaster. By giving their relationship firm boundaries and a clearly agreed-upon end date, Cal had struck just the right note to entice her, even if she had been hoping to stick around Last Stand after her job ended. Maybe she should have mentioned that to Cal—about her hope to find work on the farm after her job with his mother was over. He'd been so upfront with her.

Sitting beside him now, back in the reserved section for Last Stand fans, Josie was aware of his every movement. His every look. She could feel his gaze on her like a physical caress, and it made her wonder how she could get through two more weeks living next door to him *without* acting on his tantalizing proposal. Maybe she should just scrap her hope of staying here after the job ended and throw herself into a wild affair with Cal for the rest of her time here.

Seize whatever happiness she could while she had the chance.

She'd forced herself to pay attention to Nate's final at-bat of the evening when he struck out looking, which was apparently some sort of unforgivable crime according to Clint Ramsey.

She tried to ignore the man's loud diatribe behind them, but Cal was clearly irritated by his dad's running commentary. Josie was glad when the game came to an end. Nate's team won by two runs, sending the home team off the field early. Cal's dad left the party deck, hands shoved in his trouser pockets, his head down, while his much younger bride hurried after him in shoes that would have twisted Josie's ankles within ten steps.

"There's a happy surprise," Cal muttered darkly, watching them leave. He withdrew his phone and started texting. "I'm letting Nate know the coast is clear if he wants to meet us here."

"He must not have his phone on the field," Josie observed, pointing to where his brother stood talking to a couple of teammates near third base.

A couple of their players were being interviewed by media outlets—or at least that's what she guessed the camera crews meant. Music played over the stadium speakers while the majority of fans left the bleachers to find their vehicles. Closer to Josie and Cal on the party deck, Nate's friends and supporters were moving toward the railing, waiting their turn to say hello.

"You're right," Cal agreed, pocketing the phone and moving closer to the railing with her. "I thought he might return to the clubhouse before he came up to the stands." He peered around the deck full of Last Stand residents waving T-shirts and hats for the players to sign. "I know he's anxious to see one friend in particular."

"Right." Josie remembered hearing Nate mention a woman's name in that phone call she'd heard between them in Cal's car. "Who is Keely Harper?"

"An old girlfriend of his." His flat voice told Josie what he thought of her.

"And that's a problem because...?" Curious to learn more about the Ramsey men's romantic relationships, she was intrigued.

"Keely broke things off with him as soon as he signed a contract," he said in a low tone for her ears only. "Between you and me, I'm pretty sure she broke his heart. So for her to show up now when he stands a chance of getting into the big league—"

He shrugged, letting the observation dangle unfinished.

"You think she's after his money?"

"Possibly. The jump from minor league to major league

pay is fairly staggering. Baseball keeps its minor leaguers earning just over minimum wage, while the players at the highest level are some of the best paid athletes in the world." Cal frowned as he scanned the fans from Last Stand, some still sitting at their tables with friends and family, some crowding near the railing. "But I don't see Keely."

"He's heading this way," Josie noted, wondering if Cal's concerns were normal older-brother protectiveness and not based in reality. She remembered how Nate had sounded in that phone call when he asked about the woman—clearly, he'd looked forward to seeing her.

She watched Nate Ramsey as he neared the bleachers, a collective shout going up from his hometown fans. Dressed in a gray-and-blue baseball jersey with blue pants smudged with dirt, he was tall—well over six foot—and lankier than his brother. With light brown hair and dark brown eyes, he had an infectious grin and an easy, loping walk. She could see him catch his brother's eye right away, although he turned his attention to signing balls and T-shirts for the kids first and foremost. He had a kind word for everyone as he passed back programs and gloves, thanking parents for coming.

"He seems like a charmer," Josie whispered to Cal when his brother was almost done signing.

"He may be a changeling," Cal joked, although his pride in his sibling was evident in his voice. "He's definitely the most likable Ramsey."

Josie frowned. "I'd still pick you," she assured him. "And

is that fair to your youngest brother?"

"Wes is the best ballplayer, and that comes with its own rewards, believe me," Cal told her drily, palming her back to nudge her forward now that Nate had finished signing. "Come on. I'll introduce you."

Her skin tingled where he touched her, reminding her she had a serious decision ahead of her where this man was concerned. Did she want to take him up on his offer of a two-week affair? Her heart sped faster while the brothers clasped hands.

"Hello, Brother," Nate greeted him, scaling the wall with the railing using his long legs.

Cal kept hold of his hand, tugging him up and over, onto the deck just above field level. "Good game, Nate. Sweet double."

"Overshadowed by the strikeout, no doubt," he said grimly as his brown eyes swept the reserved area. "I see Dad was too disgusted to stick around and berate me?"

"Lucky you." Cal turned to her. "Josie, my brother Nathan." And to his brother: "Nate, this is Mom's caretaker, Josie Vance."

Really? He was introducing her as the caretaker? She smiled on autopilot and shook Nate's hand. She must not have hidden her dismay very well because Nate shook his head and grinned at her.

"Don't mind my brother," he counseled her. "He's the master of understatement. It's nice to meet you."

The brief stab of disappointment faded as she acknowledged that she hadn't given Cal any reason to introduce her as more than that. Hadn't she been adamant about keeping boundaries in place? Her reaction told her more about how much she was feeling for him—a warning sign she should probably examine more carefully.

The brothers talked briefly about their grandfather's health, making Josie realize that Cal must have brought his siblings up to speed about Everett's accident. A moment later, Nate backed up a step to get a better view of the thinning crowd on the party deck.

"So where's Keely?" he asked, scratching a hand across the stitched lettering of his jersey.

"I haven't seen her all evening," Cal admitted. "Looks like her presence tonight was just a rumor."

Nate went perfectly still, his expression changing. Josie turned to follow his gaze, curious.

"I think I see her," Nate said, already moving in that direction, higher up the bleachers. "Josie, it was great meeting you, and thanks to you both for coming."

With the help of the bright stadium lights, Josie spotted a delicate blonde in a long red sweater—visible only from the back—disappearing through an exit. She saw Nate's long legs take the steps two at a time to reach her, but she had a solid head start.

Beside her, Cal scowled. "Relationships 101—never chase a woman who doesn't want to be caught."

"But maybe you don't know their whole story," Josie protested, thinking Nate Ramsey was too likable to focus his attentions where they weren't wanted. "They could be on the verge of a beautiful romance."

"Or Nate could be on his way to heartache number two at the hands of the same woman who dished it out the first time." Cal shook his head and gripped the railing overlooking the baseball field. "Damn it."

"What's wrong?" She joined him at the railing, where Cal stared at a film crew with lights focused on...

His father.

Clint Ramsey stood in the middle of a circle of microphones and cameras, although only one was an actual film camera. The rest were smartphones. As they watched, the extra spotlight shut off and the group as a whole moved in the direction of the party deck.

"We need to get out of here," Cal informed her, his voice curt as he turned her toward the exit. "Now."

"Why?" Confused, she wondered what Cal knew that she didn't.

"My dad's out of baseball now, so the only real carrot he can dangle in front of sports journalists is an interview with one of his sons," Cal explained, guiding her down the metal steps that would take them away from the bleachers. "And since Nate is already on the other side of the stadium to chase after an old flame, that leaves me."

Josie missed a step. If Cal hadn't caught her with lightning-quick reflexes, she would have slid down the rest of the stairs.

"You think they're coming to interview you?" It had never occurred to her there might be media at a game like this who would be interested in Cal's career, but that had been shortsighted of her.

Panic rose, her throat going tight. She couldn't afford to get caught on camera. She'd been so careful to choose a sleepy Texas town for her caretaking job, far from her Florida hometown and the mess she'd left behind. Far from her mother's threats that she had willfully ignored because she hadn't wanted to imagine her mom would be truly vindictive toward her.

Even as Cal righted her, a bright light popped on in front of her, all but blinding her. A microphone entered her field of vision while a disembodied voice boomed, "Cal Ramsey, care to comment on your status in the league?"

Struck speechless, Josie gripped Cal's arm like her life depended on it. She ducked her head and followed him fast, praying she didn't end up on camera.

"This is Nate's night," Cal told them as they reached the bottom of the stairs. Then he pivoted her sharply in the other direction. "I couldn't be more proud of my brothers," he called to them even as he hustled her out of the limelight and toward the hallway where his security friend had greeted them earlier.

The security guard waved Cal and Josie through before planting himself in front of the cameras.

"Come on," Cal urged in her ear, leading her through one of the offices and into a hallway they hadn't been in before. "We can get to the parking lot through here. I'm taking you home."

Her heart raced. And this time, it wasn't with anticipation of a possible night with Cal—even though she'd been seriously debating it. Now, she was just flat-out scared.

Because if someone from her hometown saw her on the arm of a famous baseball player, her peaceful days in Last Stand were over.

Chapter Eight

T HE RIDE BACK to Last Stand had been tense. Cal had dodged repeated calls from his father and a handful of media outlets, but he'd felt compelled to respond when his agent phoned. Not that he wanted to discuss his stalled career, but he'd ignored enough of his agent's calls in the rough weeks after he was designated for assignment. He owed the guy an explanation for how he'd ended up in front of the camera at a minor league park. Dex had assured him he would keep an ear out for any media mentions, and that conversation had helped Cal's mood turn a corner.

No thanks to his dad.

Now, Cal pulled into the gravel road between the farmhouse and the two-story garage where he'd been spending his nights. He'd had high hopes for this night with Josie, but she'd seemed as rattled by the media sneak attack as him, turning quiet on the ride home. That upset him more than anything else about his father's tactics to keep Cal in the spotlight. Because more than anything, Cal wanted to end this night with Josie. To pick up where that kiss had left off back at the stadium.

"Are you okay?" he asked, parking the vehicle and shutting down the engine. "I know we didn't have the best end to the evening."

It had taken him the first half of the trip home just to get a handle on the anger he felt toward his father. Because it was one thing to offer unsolicited career advice or trash-talk his sons' talents. Those things were par for the course with Dad. But to shine the media spotlight on Cal at the lowest point in his career was just wrong, even for him. And that didn't even begin to address his frustration for Josie's sake. He'd wanted her to have fun tonight, not spend the evening dodging interviews.

"I'm fine. Getting cornered by the cameras was just surprising." She met his gaze across the front seat of his car. "Is that common for you?"

"No." He shook his head before opening the driver's side door and coming around to help her out of the vehicle. He might have been distracted most of the way home, but he could salvage some semblance of manners now. "Even after one of my own games, I wouldn't be on camera unless I had a significant impact on the game."

Which last year—when he'd been hitting well—had been a surprising number of times. Remembering about how quick the team was to release him this year in spite of that, he felt a fresh wave of frustration as he walked Josie to the front door. How differently this night might have ended if he could have avoided the journalists.

"Do you know who was filming?" She unlocked the front door and let the dogs out, standing aside as the three of them raced past in a chorus of happy barks. The littlest one did a bonus dance around their feet before running to catch up with the others. "Was it just the in-house camera crew that takes footage of all the games?"

"No." He guessed she meant the cameras that picked up the closed-circuit coverage of each game. "The interviewer who passed the microphone our way is with the regional sports network that covers all of the Texas teams."

She tucked her keys back into the fabric bag she carried, then set the sack just inside the open door to the house while they waited for the dogs to return. At least, he assumed that's what she was waiting for. If there was any chance they could salvage this night together, he planned to be here to see it through. Hell, a night with her could smooth over all the rough edges of this day, allowing him to forget everything but the pleasure of her touch.

Her kiss.

Memories of it roared back to life with a vengeance as he watched her in the moonlight. A breeze made the night temperature bearable, the air wafting the scent of peaches from one of the fruit trees on the far side of the garden.

"But since you didn't answer their questions, the clip is unlikely to be broadcast anywhere, right?" She gave an awkward shrug, the movement sliding her T-shirt along her curves. "Just curious how many people will see my ungainly stumble down the stadium stairs."

"Most likely no one," he assured her, not sure how to read her body language. She seemed nervous, and that bothered him. Was it because of him? Or was she worried about the possibility of being on camera? "I'm hardly a news story these days, especially around here."

It would be one thing if any teams had approached his agent about him, but if no one had any interest in acquiring him, he was truly out of the game for good. He still hadn't wrapped his head around what that meant. Because—family drama about the sport aside—Cal loved baseball.

"So why would they have put the camera on you in the first place?" She folded her arms and peered up at him, eyes searching him.

What answers was she looking for? What was holding her back from acting on the attraction they'd talked of exploring?

He wasn't sure of anything except that he would give her whatever she wanted if that meant they could end this hellish night in bed together.

"My father's a Texas baseball legend and he's been the Ramsey family's P.R. machine since we were in high school. For all his faults, he's very well liked by the media." There had been a time—long ago—when Cal had appreciated that. Back before criticism became his dad's main form of communication. Before Clint had betrayed Cal's mom. "There aren't many fathers who've raised multiple sons to play in the league. So that's an easy angle for him to tout whenever he wants to stir up some press."

She nodded as she seemed to think it over, but there was a nervous tic beneath one eye, so subtle he might have missed it if he hadn't carved a spot for himself in the majors by being damned good at reading body language. Pitchers worked hard to be unreadable, but most of them had their tells in the way they held their bodies or where their eyes went before a pitch came barreling down the strike zone.

"And while I'm damn sorry that you were caught in that drama tonight, I'd like nothing better than to forget about it." He didn't want to think about his career going down in flames, and all the questions that raised. He wanted to touch her. To kiss her again and lose himself in the taste and feel of her.

But he had meant it when he said the next move was hers, so he fisted his hands at his sides and waited.

"I understand. But I have just one more question about what happened tonight." She nibbled her lip in a gesture that captivated him, his gaze fixed on the movement, heat rushing up his spine.

Hunger for her twisted painfully.

"One question," he agreed, the air between them thickening with awareness.

"You made a compelling argument for an affair earlier." She twirled the end of her braid around one finger. "I wondered if you could refresh my memory before I make up my mind?"

He couldn't remember ever being so grateful for a change of subject. More importantly, he couldn't remember ever wanting a woman as much as he wanted Josie right now. Whatever nervousness he'd thought he'd been seeing in her before, it didn't have anything to do with him or the chemistry between them.

"You're asking for a recap?" He told himself not to rush, even though he wanted to kiss her into the house and straight to the closest bed.

She'd been hurt before, and he would do everything in his power to make her feel good. Blissful, even.

His end goal was definitely bliss for both of them.

"If it's not too much trouble."

"Just the opposite." He stepped closer, his shadow falling over her while the peach-scented breeze stirred around them. "It would be my tremendous pleasure."

He cupped her shoulders to steady her. Then captured her lips with his. Testing. Tasting.

For a moment, the slug of his own heartbeat in his ears drowned out the noise of the crickets, his whole world narrowed to this moment. This woman.

When her hands crept around his neck, her body swaying in to his, it was better than any victory fireworks, more powerful than any extra innings win. He wanted to haul her against him and keep her there, feel every inch of her, but he forced himself to break the kiss. To be sure what she wanted.

Breathing ragged, he shifted his hands to her hips. Contented himself with sketching a touch along her narrow waist. He skimmed his thumb under the hem of her T-shirt, finding a patch of bare skin just above the waist of her denim skirt.

"I run the risk of getting carried away when we're standing this close to a bed," he explained. "So if my persuasive skills are less eloquent, it's only because I want you so damned badly."

She kept her arms around his neck, her fingers combing lightly through his hair. She pressed against him, her back arching as she whispered, "Then it's a good thing I'm already thoroughly persuaded."

JOSIE KNEW SHE took a risk getting close to Cal. But she wanted to take it. Take this night. Take him. Before the world might possibly blow up in her face.

He'd given her the opportunity to reason her way through to the decision, letting her think about it on the drive back to Last Stand from San Antonio. And while she was nervous about the possibility that she'd been on camera tonight, and scared about her future with no job lined up after her caretaking gig, she still wanted this time with a man who'd treated her respectfully. Sweetly. Thoughtfully.

She needed this night.

Needed him.

Cal kissed her, letting her feel his hunger in a way that made her understand he'd been holding back before. Closing her eyes, she gave herself over to the moment, breathing him in. His hands molded her, fitting her against him, stirring her senses everywhere he touched.

His ragged groan vibrated through his chest and hers too. Her breasts beaded, desire making her skin feel tight. She pressed closer, sealing her hips to his and finding him very ready to give her everything she needed.

"We should go inside," he said in a rush, like a drowning man suddenly coming up for air. "I'll get the dogs."

Her body buzzed like she'd just gotten a shock, everything humming and vibrantly alive.

"Okay," she eked out the word through a dry throat, her thoughts filled with images of her and Cal together.

Naked.

Stumbling into the farmhouse's living room, she moved her bag to a kitchen chair and flicked on the hallway light while Cal whistled for the dogs. She checked their water dishes and saw they were all set for the night. As an afterthought, she pulled two bottled waters from the refrigerator. Cracking one open, she sipped it as Cal locked the front door once the animals were inside.

The Labs gladly found their beds in the mudroom, huffing deep breaths as they dropped into their favorite spots. Kungfu glanced up at the couch and then back at her, clearly debating how much to push her luck.

"It's not my rule," she reminded the Maltipoo, passing one of the water bottles to Cal before shooing the little dog toward her open crate tricked out with her favorite toys. "But we both have to follow it."

"You don't need to close her in there?" Cal asked while Josie flipped a sheet over the whole contraption with the door still open.

"Oddly, no. Your mom told me she likes the sheet trick,

and sure enough, Kungfu stays in there most nights." Straightening, she fell right into Cal's hot gaze.

"It seems like everyone is tucked in now." Cal took a long drink from the bottle she'd given him, then set it aside on a low table between the mudroom and the living area. "Except for you and me."

Her heart pounded so loudly he must surely hear it. The sound of it filled her ears as she looked over him, this supremely attractive man wrapped in enviable muscle and sex appeal. His shadowed jaw called to her fingers, his green eyes making her smolder as he watched her.

"I don't feel the least bit tired," she observed, her hands drawn to his body, running over his chest and shoulders. "Far from it."

A smile played around his lips while his muscles shifted under her palms.

"Nevertheless, we should find a bed." He wrapped her in strong arms. Lifted her. "You'll want to be comfortable when I'm taking your clothes off."

The thrill that shot through her made her shiver, gave her the distraction she so deeply craved. He walked her through the house toward the bedroom he'd slept in the one night they'd spent under the same roof. Carried her upstairs.

As he moved, his hips shifted against hers creating the hottest friction imaginable. Well, maybe not *imaginable* since she could envision an even hotter kind of contact. But she hadn't expected her body to hurtle toward orgasm territory so quickly.

When he stepped into the large guest suite, he gently lowered her to her feet again. The room was dark with the blinds closed, but a light from the hall filtered in through the door he'd left partially open. She'd hardly been in this room since he'd made the bed after the one night he'd spent here. The comforter on the king-sized platform bed was a subdued gray, the furnishings spare in a minimalist way. She remembered a big painting of the farmhouse took up one wall, and windows filled two of the others. A ceiling fan turned silently from one of the exposed beams, sending a rush of cool air over her warm skin as they regarded each other.

"It's sweet of you to offer to undress me." She remembered his words about taking her clothes off, but the trip up the stairs made her realize she needed to act fast this first time. To capitalize on the moment. "But it occurs to me the process will be more efficient if we each tackle our own garments."

Before she lost her nerve, she gripped the hem of her T-shirt and tugged it up and off.

Her boldness was rewarded by the heat in his gaze. She had his rapt attention.

"Josie." He whispered her name in a lingering way that gave it an extra syllable. "Hell."

"Now it's your turn." She wouldn't have the nerve to strip all the way unless he started shedding some clothes too. For incentive's sake. "Let me see you."

His T-shirt came off like a magic trick, one hand yanking and then—*poof*—it was on the floor. She was pretty sure he never took his eyes off her. But then she may have gotten distracted by all that sharply delineated muscle. From his mouth-watering deltoids and biceps, to his rigid abs and sexy-as-sin obliques, she said a prayer of thanksgiving for the man's commitment to working out. Because…wow. He'd earned that body.

"Maybe I was wrong," she murmured, half to herself, as she reached out to stroke her palm down the center of his pecs.

"About what?" he asked, slipping a finger under one bright blue bra strap. Flicking it off her shoulder.

"About it being more efficient to undress ourselves." She placed a kiss on his chest. Then licked the spot she'd kissed. "I'm getting seriously distracted."

She couldn't decide where she wanted to taste him next. The options were plentiful, and all so appealing.

"Then maybe you should allow me to take over." His arm wound around her back to flick open the hooks on her bra before he pulled the silky fabric off her completely. "As a professional athlete, I've had to hone a laser focus."

She felt light-headed when he cupped her breasts, bending to kiss one taut peak and then the other. But, true to his word, he kept his hands moving, unfastening her skirt and stripping away the rest of her clothes in a blink. Naked in his arms, she didn't protest when he lifted her up again, depositing her in the center of the bed. He disappeared for a moment, returning from the bathroom with a condom packet and no clothes.

No. Damned. Clothes.

She levered up on her elbows to better survey the display of powerful masculinity, but she didn't have much time to take him in before he stretched out over her on the bed. Falling back against the pillows, she lost herself in a sensual collide of bodies, every place where they touched a delicious revelation. His thigh slid between hers and she forgot everything but how much she wanted him.

Breathless, she twined her arms around his neck, shamelessly rocking against him. He kissed his way from her lips down her neck, the soft rasp of his jaw gently abrading her skin. She combed her fingers through his dark hair, her body keenly attuned to his roaming hands and wicked mouth. As his kisses trailed lower, she thought she might unravel just from the promise of what was to come.

"I'm already so close," she warned him, feeling all the urgency between her hips. "So maybe we should—"

He kissed her mouth slowly, quieting the thought, before he answered. "There's no limit to the number of orgasms you can have."

She might have laughed at the joy of that statement, except he chose that moment to tease a featherlight touch along her slick heat, sending her hurtling toward her release.

The silky sweet shock of it had her gasping, clinging to him as she rode the pleasure of all those microbursts of sensation—one after the other. Lights flashed behind her eyelids, the spasms of her completion giving her muscles the sweetest possible workout. When the last tremor eased and she finally relaxed back against the mattress, she pried her eyes open to see Cal's face over hers, outlined by the light from the hall.

"Laser focus indeed," she managed, cupping his jaw in one hand and stroking his rough cheek with her thumb.

He was already rolling the condom into place, the shift of his muscles tantalizing her all over again. Pleasurable tension pulled tight once more, her back arching to get close to him.

To Cal.

She watched as his green eyes narrowed, his attention on her while he eased inside her. Robbing her of her thought. Igniting her from the inside out.

Her fingers clenched into his shoulders, legs wrapping around his waist. Gazes locked, they met thrust for thrust, the pleasure building all over again for her. Pressing closer, she kissed him, rolling him to his back so she had more control. Wanting to make him feel every bit as amazing as she had.

Staring down at him, she watched the shadows play over his face as she moved with him, getting a feel for what he liked best. She rolled her hips slowly. And then faster, finding her rhythm.

"Slower," he urged her, his strong hands capturing her waist and holding her there for a long moment, until she leaned down to whisper in his ear.

"There's no limit to the number of times I can make you feel good," she reminded him.

She felt the way his body tensed, hands squeezing her harder, for all of a moment before his release pounded through him. He gripped her hips, burying himself deeper inside her, and the movement sent her over the edge with him, her body convulsing with his.

In the aftermath, she wound up lying by his side, not entirely sure how she got there. Their breath mingled in the cool room, legs still tangled as he drew a quilt over them both. She tucked the cotton binding under her chin and tipped her forehead to his chest, listening to the sound of his heartbeat, comforted by it somehow, even though she knew they'd just waded into dangerous romantic terrain by getting intimate.

Especially considering the risk she'd taken by going to the game tonight and being photographed with Cal. What if it led her mother to Last Stand? Or the police?

She knew she needed to tie up her work in Texas and move on. Her hopes of securing a job here had been formed too soon, before this misstep of landing on camera with a sports star. But she felt too amazing to worry about that right now.

Somehow, she would figure out a place to go next. Some place as quiet and remote as Last Stand. What concerned her most in those heady moments after the best sex of her life was how she would walk away from this man in just two short weeks.

Chapter Nine

C AL DIDN'T WANT to leave Josie's side the next morning. She looked so damned beautiful with the rays of dawn slanting through the blinds to light her face in a shade of golden pink. They'd kept one another awake for more of the night than they'd slept, though. He figured he owed it to her to let her catch up on rest while he went for his run.

What an incredible night they'd shared. In spite of the nervousness he'd thought he'd glimpsed in her earlier in the evening, she'd seemed happy once she'd made the decision to invite him in. He hoped she would wake up just as happy, because he wanted to spend as much time with her as he could over the next two weeks.

Kissing her forehead, he slid from under the covers and left her a note promising to cook her a late breakfast. Then he dug out an old pair of running shorts from a dresser containing an odd assortment of his old clothes from other times he'd returned to Last Stand.

Not often enough, he realized.

As he found a pair of earbuds and cranked the tunes, he let the dogs out for a few minutes so they wouldn't wake Josie. Then, locking the house behind him, he hit one of the dirt roads around the old barns that led to the farm and orchards, taking in the beauty of a place he hadn't made much time for in the last few years.

Feet pounding an even rhythm, he passed the empty stalls no longer used since Rough Hollow Ranch became Rough Hollow Farm and Orchards. Everett had turned the failing ranch into a profitable enterprise by planting peach trees. The capital he'd gained from selling off the last of the livestock had given him enough to invest in the new operation. Had his father been angry with him for turning his back on ranching, a long-held Ramsey tradition? Cal didn't know. There was too much he didn't understand about the family history after a lifetime commitment to baseball—the new Ramsey tradition, he thought drily.

Yet after hearing the gratitude in his grandfather's voice the one time that Cal had checked out the orchards for him, he understood how much that land continued to mean to him. Clint had made it clear that if his father passed the farming operation to him, he would sell it off without hesitation. So if they wanted to keep Rough Hollow in the family, a Ramsey needed to move back to Last Stand. If no one picked up Cal's contract, of course, he was the logical candidate. He wouldn't disrupt his brothers' careers if his own came to a natural—albeit unwanted—end.

On the other hand, if a team picked him up, Cal would go back to the game—no question. He loved the game. He already missed it like crazy.

Then, he'd try to convince Nate or Wes to at least spend

the off-season here to reconnect with the place. Test out how it would feel to take on Rough Hollow.

Sun rising higher, the peach orchards were heavily fragrant as the day grew hotter. Cal spotted a tree in one of the old orchards where remnants of an old fort rotted among the branches. He slowed his step to check out the missing rungs on the ladder up to a long-ago hideout he'd built with his brothers. No doubt they weren't supposed to make forts in trees that provided produce for the farm stand, but Everett hadn't minded. Their grandfather—after seeing their early efforts at building a tree house—even provided milled lumber and a battery-operated power drill that had kept them occupied for days.

That was back when their father was still in the game. He'd been a pitching coach after he'd retired as a player, unable to tear himself away from the sport. But once he'd sat on the sidelines of one of Wes's T-ball games and seen the quality of his youngest son's swing, he'd given up his job to devote himself to being a full-time coach to Cal, Nate and Wes. That's when things had started getting tense. Cal, at least, had known a few years of normalcy before that day. Wes hardly remembered a time without daily skills drills.

Tugging out his earbuds, Cal climbed the remaining rungs to peer inside the tree house, surprised his grandfather hadn't burned this section of orchard and replanted the field. Even the variety of peach tree was different from the kinds he harvested now—all compact hybrids with high yield. This tree was big and broad, gnarled branches twisting around the simply constructed house with four windows, a drop-down door, and all the siblings' names carved in the wood.

His cell phone ringing pulled him out of the past. He connected the call as he climbed back down, the screen showing his agent's number.

Tension pulled his shoulders tight.

"Hey, Dex. What's up?" He swiped a hand across his forehead, walking along the dirt path. He pulled a peach off one of the old trees and searched it carefully for defects before taking a bite.

The explosion of sweetness on his tongue helped relax him just a fraction while his agent, Dexter Brantley, spoke.

"Hi, Cal. I know you said you're not interested in hearing from me unless I have concrete news," Dex began, clearly remembering Cal's frustration about phone calls just to "touch base" with him. "But I wanted you to know that I heard from Dusty Reed last night."

Cal stopped walking, peach juice still dripping from his chin. He swiped that away with the back of his hand, thoughts racing. His father had mentioned Dusty—one of Cal's former coaches—was getting back in baseball.

"And?" He hadn't checked his phone today to see if there'd been any industry news. Had Dusty taken a new position?

"He was cagey about where he's going, but I have every reason to think he's close to locking down a move to either Oakland or Arizona." As an agent to athletes at every level in nearly every sport, Dex kept his eye on industry news and he had contacts everywhere. If he didn't know where Dusty was going, no one else knew either.

"Interesting," Cal acknowledged as he kept walking, his thoughts straying back to Josie sleeping in the farmhouse. He hadn't told her much about his career, preferring not to talk about something that pained him. Yet he found himself wanting to talk to her now. To share his worries about what to do next. "But I don't see how that affects me."

He refused to think about things that "might" happen.

"It wouldn't," Dex continued, raising his voice to be heard over the background noise of a busy city—a loud siren must have passed close by where he was standing. "Except Dusty was calling to check the details of your contract and availability."

Cal stopped again. There was no way the guy would go to that level of trouble unless he knew full well he'd be running his own team again soon.

"Meaning he might lobby his new general manager to sign me if he firms up a deal with a team." Many teams didn't allow the manager to make those kinds of personnel decisions, but sometimes wily veterans made those picks part of their negotiations for the job. It wasn't uncommon for a new manager to lobby for assistant managers or trainers so they could surround themselves with a staff they knew would work well together.

But it was less likely Dusty would have that kind of sway for anyone in the lineup.

"I'm sure he's already solidified an agreement with a

team if he made that call to me—it just hasn't been made public yet for whatever reason," Dex confirmed, the siren in the background fading. "My guess is that he's headed to Oakland since I can see that front office giving him a little more wiggle room to make suggestions for the lineup." Dex delved deeper into the West Coast team's inner workings, but Cal was already thinking about what a move like that would mean for him personally.

A whole hell of a lot.

There was a chance his career wasn't ending this season. An opportunity to make a difference to a team with the only real skill he possessed. He took another bite of his peach, already committing himself to a longer run. He could still keep his word to make Josie a late breakfast. Only now, he'd have good news to share.

"So what does your gut say?" he asked Dex, a new spring in his step as he walked through the quiet old orchard. "How soon do you think we'll hear the news that Dusty signed on to manage a club?"

He didn't ask the other question that he really wanted an answer to—how much longer would it be until Dusty's new team contacted Cal's agent?

"I would think we'll hear the announcement within a few days—a week at the very most." Dex hesitated. "After that, I would hope we'd hear from the new management within twenty-four hours."

Right. Which meant if three days went by with no word from the team, Cal wasn't getting an offer. He appreciated the agent's candor.

"Thanks, Dex." Cal was ready to disconnect when the next words stopped him.

"One more thing, Cal," Dex added, lowering his voice as the background noise faded completely. Perhaps he'd stepped indoors. "This probably goes without saying since you've never been outspoken with the media or inclined to get into trouble, but you're aware Dusty is a very straight arrow who doesn't appreciate bad publicity, right?"

"Very aware." Cal laughed, remembering the way the old-school manager ran a team. "As someone raised under the Clint Ramsey school of discipline, that won't be a problem."

Cal had learned early not to put a toe out of line with his father. Dusty had been vocal about appreciating what Cal brought to the clubhouse the last time he'd played for the manager. He was a stabilizing influence for the younger guys. He'd never minded that role since it was the same one he'd always had in his own family.

Ending the call, Cal put his earbuds back in and continued his run, more optimistic than he'd been in a month. But even as he looked forward to hearing from a new team, he selfishly hoped that call wouldn't come for two more weeks.

Because as much as he wanted to get back to his game, he wanted Josie too. It surprised him to realize just how much.

WAKING TO THE scent of bacon from the kitchen, Josie stretched sleepily, thinking a woman could get used to this. Great sex with a thoughtful, caring man, followed by sleeping late and having breakfast prepared for her. She jumped in the shower before padding back to her own bedroom to find clean clothes.

By the time she went downstairs, Cal was pouring them both coffee, two places set at the table in the breakfast nook. The simple white farmhouse china was pretty against a gingham tablecloth, reminding her how little energy she'd put into feeding herself for the past two months. Between trying to live frugally, and not wanting to use too many of Hailey Decker's things, Josie had tended to eat fresh fruit and vegetables at the bar. But clearly, Cal wanted to have a nicer meal than that. His hair was damp, his broad shoulders filling out a well-worn T-shirt. A pair of faded jeans rode low on his hips.

A thrill shot through her as their gazes connected. Distractedly, she greeted the dogs as they circled her, tails wagging.

"Good morning," Cal greeted her, setting down the coffeepot to pull her against him.

He kissed her thoroughly, long enough to make her forget about breakfast.

"I hope you're hungry," he said into her ear before he

pulled away.

"Definitely." She couldn't hide the pleasurable shiver that went through her even as she remembered some of the things she'd been worried about last night.

She'd been so focused on the scent of bacon and the happiness of going to sleep in Cal's arms the night before, she hadn't given any thought to the fact that her cover might be blown in Last Stand. What if someone from her hometown had seen the image of her with Cal? A knot of worry pulled tight in her belly as Cal pulled out her chair for her and then took the seat across the table.

"I had some potentially encouraging news this morning," he told her, passing her the platter of scrambled eggs while he helped himself to the bacon.

"Really?" She wondered what it would be like to have a normal relationship with a good man like Cal Ramsey.

Did other people sit across the breakfast table and talk about what was going on in their lives? It must be nice to have someone to share things with. To not feel like there were too many secrets to keep all the time.

Josie had spent so much of her life hiding the ugliness of her mother's landlord practices from the tenants and—conversely—hiding all the work she did for the tenants from her mother. She hadn't realized how thoroughly the stress had exhausted her until she'd come to Last Stand and had time away from it. Her stomach hadn't stopped churning for two weeks.

"My agent called to let me know one of my old managers—a guy who thought well of me—is being hired by one of the major league teams." He exchanged his platter of bacon for the eggs and kept filling his plate.

Josie sipped from her coffee. "And you think this person might bring you back into baseball?"

She understood little about his sport and even less about the business behind the sport, but she could see he seemed hopeful. Upbeat.

"There's a chance. Managers don't have the power to make roster changes, but since he's coming into this position because the club is struggling to begin with, he probably discussed team personnel at length with the head of baseball operations. It's possible he lobbied for me to have a place in the lineup." He grinned at her over his orange juice glass. "I'm not counting on it by a long shot, but it's the only positive career news I've had in a month."

"That's exciting." Even though having Cal back on a baseball team meant he would leave Last Stand, it was obvious how important the game was in his life. "It's a good thing your mother will be returning soon since Everett might be disappointed to have both of us leave town at once."

She regretted bringing that up since it made Cal's smile fade. His brow furrowed while he buttered a slice of whole-grain toast.

"No doubt. I was thinking about him and the family situation with Rough Hollow this morning." He set down the knife and the toast too, sounding frustrated. "I hate for his sake that none of his grandkids are stepping up to take over the business. It feels disloyal of us."

"Your father wouldn't take over the farm until you or one or your brothers retires from baseball?" She took another bite of her eggs, wondering how Cal and his siblings would feel about selling the business outside the family. "I mean, there must be a limited number of years that a player can compete—" She stopped herself midsentence, realizing how that observation might sting a man already grappling with the possible end of his career. She didn't mean to dim his new hope for a return. "That is—"

"I know what you mean." He nodded as he passed a slice of bacon to each of the dogs, seeming unfazed. "I think the average time in the major league hovers around five or six years. But that counts a lot of guys who only have a game or two under their belts. My father's career as a player spanned seventeen seasons."

"Wow, that's incredible. So there's a chance you and your brothers will be playing for another decade." She suspected that was too long a time for Clint Ramsey to run a farming business. But then, maybe that idea hadn't made sense in the first place. She didn't really know how much time and expertise it took to run that kind of operation. "I notice you don't talk much about your sister. There's no chance she'd want to—"

Cal was already shaking his head. "Lara made it clear she'll never live in Last Stand again."

She wanted to ask why, but she also didn't want to push for too many details when she still kept a lock on her own past.

"I'm sorry that I brought up the future of the farm on a day of good news for you." She set aside her fork and reached across the table to squeeze his forearm. "You must be looking forward to a fresh start."

"If it all comes together." His green eyes met hers and she felt the simmer of their connection tingle through her. "And either way, I'm hoping I don't hear for a little while longer so we can enjoy these two weeks together."

Awareness heated her skin. Clearly he looked forward to that time as much as she did. It caught her off guard to know that this successful, smart, gorgeous man felt that way about her.

"I'd like that, too," she admitted, wondering how she'd get her chores done each day with the lure of this man nearby. Even now she was wondering how fast they could finish breakfast so they could tear each other's clothes off again.

"The funny part about my agent's call was that he felt the need to warn me to be on good behavior until we hear from a new team." Cal's eyes lit with humor while Josie's belly knotted with worry. "As if I could get into any trouble touring the orchards and painting Everett's house. Obviously, my agent has never been to Last Stand."

Her appetite vanished at the thought of her past rearing its ugly head at a time that could hurt Cal's return to baseball.

"He should know you better than that." Anxiety made it

hard for her to stay in her seat at the table. Suddenly, she couldn't help but hope Cal's call came sooner rather than later, even if it meant robbing her of time with the worthiest man she'd ever met.

"He does. But I'm sure he's seen a lot of contracts vanish for the sake of a single poor decision." Cal stood to retrieve the coffeepot and top off their drinks.

He must not have noticed her nervousness when he dropped a kiss on her head as he filled her cup. She wanted to lean in to him, to close her eyes and take comfort in his strong presence, but the sense of guilt over keeping her past a secret was eating away at her.

She debated sharing the truth right then. To just put it out there and see if he thought it was a cause for concern, since forewarned was forearmed. Even if it meant losing him for good. She had to be honest.

"Cal—" She traced the pattern on the handle of her spoon, figuring the only way to tell him was to just start talking.

His cell phone vibrated, interrupting her.

Her gaze flew to his, and she noticed the way he winked at her. Like they shared a happy secret. Like he might be receiving good news.

Except, when he flipped over his phone and checked the message, she could tell by his expression that it was anything but. His face went blank.

She hugged her arms around herself, praying the news didn't have anything to do with her. Knowing it damn well did.

"Cal?" Her voice was a thin rasp. "Is everything okay?"

He slid his phone across the table to her, screen side up. "See for yourself."

The coldness in his words was a clear warning.

Her gaze went to a photo from the game last night, her turning in to Cal's arm as he scowled at whoever was taking their photograph. But the damning part was the caption beneath the image.

Released from his contract, former Rebels player Calvin Ramsey steps out with a Florida woman currently under police investigation.

Her stomach sank to her toes. She grappled for words and failed, her whole world feeling off-kilter.

What had she done?

Cal's voice sounded like a stranger's when he spoke again. "I think you owe me an explanation."

Chapter Ten

H ER RESPONSE WAS damning. The blood had drained from her face and she struggled to speak.

Was it *true*?

Cal's agent had sent him the image and caption from one of the more sleazy blogs that followed baseball players' personal lives—a blog he wouldn't have checked himself if Dex hadn't texted it to him with a question mark. His first instinct had been to think it must be clickbait—a lie with no relation to the truth. But Josie's white face and failure to speak had told him otherwise.

He'd known she was keeping secrets. But not in a million years would he have guessed she'd withhold that kind of bombshell from him. From his *mother*, for crying out loud, who'd hired her. How could she betray his trust this way? What did that say about her character?

And if she'd cost him his chance at a career comeback?

He couldn't even comprehend that kind of sucker punch coming from a woman he'd started to care for. He took his phone back from her, shutting off the screen. The image hadn't appeared anywhere with a big media reach, but little clickbait images like this could turn into major problems within hours in the current culture of social media sharing. He'd seen it happen to plenty of other athletes, and he'd always wondered how a player could put himself in that kind of position.

"It's not what you think." She leaned toward him, her fingers touching his arm, but he pulled back, still reeling from this news.

He'd felt a moment's regret at hurting her, but damn it, he needed answers if he was going to get on top of a potential scandal.

"I don't know what I think, and that's not an explanation." Anger roiled, hot and fast, an acidic churn in his gut.

Hurt lurked underneath the anger, but he tamped that down. Wouldn't acknowledge it when she'd played him so completely.

"I didn't think she'd really turned me in," she said softly, more to herself. Arms wrapped around her midsection, she moved to a window overlooking the garden, her blue eyes focused on some distant point. "I hoped she was just bluffing."

One of the Labs—he couldn't keep them straight— ducked its head under her palm and nosed at Josie's thigh, whimpering sympathetically.

Cal didn't share the empathy. His jaw clenched so hard he risked his back teeth. Why hadn't Josie simply denied it, if wasn't true? The answer seemed obvious. Painful.

He rose to his feet but remained in the middle of the kitchen, not going near her for fear some of his unwanted feelings would get the better of him.

"Would it be easier if I phoned the police and asked them to shed some light on the situation?" He was direct. To the point.

Because he needed answers now. If his career was going to tank, he wanted to know what he'd be facing in the firestorm to come.

She took a deep breath and turned wounded eyes on him, but something in his expression made her spine snap straight again. Whatever vulnerability he'd glimpsed in her vanished.

"My last employer—my mother—owns a building of low-income apartments where I have long held the unenviable position of building supervisor." She dragged in a breath, pinching the bridge of her nose for a moment, as if to ward off a pain before stroking the Lab's head with her fingers. "I have zero budget to address tenant concerns thanks to my mother's habit of spending more than she makes. Which means I am often in the position of fixing things with more duct tape and ingenuity than actual resources."

"Go on." So far, it sounded believable. He remembered her ease with the ceiling fan he'd installed. Still, he kept his distance. Not trusting himself to move too close to her and fall victim to the tempting scent of her.

"I do the best I can for the tenants on limited resources. When an eighty-five-year-old widow on a respirator calls me because her air conditioning doesn't work, believe me, I'm motivated to get it up and running for her, even though my mother's typical response is something like, 'well, no one else is complaining.'" Her blue eyes flashed grit and determination, her shoulders tense. And then she huffed out a sigh and leaned back against the window frame. "But I'm not a licensed contractor for that kind of work."

He'd heard that contracting without a license was a bigger deal in some states than others, but he hadn't been aware it could be prosecuted criminally. Especially for the picture that Josie was painting him, which made it sound like she'd been doing her best in an impossible situation.

Cal tried to connect the dots in her story, needing to get a handle on how far he would be dragged over hot coals for this. "And someone turned you in?"

"My mother, apparently." The words rasped from her throat with raw emotion. She shoved a hand through her curls still unruly from sleeping on them.

And he hated how much her mother's betrayal seemed to have hurt her. But could he really afford to empathize with a woman who'd let him walk into this P.R. nightmare with zero warning? His temples throbbed.

"But you were providing the service on her behalf, correct?" He didn't fully understand the family dynamic since she'd never talked about her mother before.

Purposely, he now guessed. She'd brushed an unhappy past under the table without considering how much a baseball player lived in the public eye. Was that his fault for not wanting to talk about the career he'd feared was over? Or hers for hiding the truth about her past?

"Yes. She was furious that I wanted to quit the job. Things did not end well between us—"

Cal wanted to be understanding. Really, he did. But her choice to gloss over this glaring detail about her past was very likely going to cost him the slim shot he'd had of making a comeback, and the anguish of that was too damned much.

"Bottom line, you knew it was a possibility that she'd file a complaint, and you went out of state to take a job with my mother to avoid the fallout." He was beginning to see the bigger picture now, and he didn't like what he saw. "Is that about right?"

Lips pursed tight, she glared at him. But finally, she spoke, her words clipped. "I left hoping she would calm down once I was gone."

"Quibbling. Either way, it's true you're being investigated, and that you hid the information from my mother and from me." The bare facts of what she'd done burned past his anger and all the way down to the hurt in his chest. Still, there was only one solution that he could see. He had to protect his mother. And, selfishly, he wanted to safeguard whatever chance he had left of salvaging his career. Given how much he'd sacrificed for it, was that too damned much to ask? Regret closed over him in a dark cloud as he realized he only had one option left in this situation. "Considering the way you've lied by omission, I think you should go."

He sure as hell hadn't wanted to end things this way. Especially not after what they'd shared the night before.

Staring back at him, she held herself motionless for a

long moment, then gave a small, jerky nod. Accepting.

"What about the dogs?" She cleared her throat and blinked fast. "The garden and bees?"

Memories of her reading the book on bees, helping his grandfather, lending her green thumb to the gardens all rolled through his head now. Losing that—losing her—hurt more than he expected, but she'd had plenty of opportunities to tell him about her past. About the possibility of bad press. Maybe if she'd given him some kind of warning, he could have taken precautions. Or not have been photographed at the game.

He couldn't play the what-if game. She hadn't told him. And now he had to do the right thing. A clean break would be easier for both of them.

"I will personally see to it that everything is cared for here until my mother returns from her mission trip." He couldn't afford to think about Josie and what she would do next, not when she'd put him in an untenable situation. He needed to phone his agent. Work on a plan for damage control before this turned into a bigger scandal.

Just in case there was any chance he could salvage a roster spot.

"And that's it?" she asked him, still standing by the window.

Now, all the dogs had moved to sit by her feet, giving her their silent support even though her actions were clearly in the wrong. Indefensible. Even if he didn't care about the legality of what she'd done, he couldn't get beyond the fact that she'd never said a word about it. That she'd allowed him to be blindsided this way.

He looked at her—ached for her—and wanted to come up with a different answer. But he knew he had to let her go.

"I don't think there's anything left to say," he informed her, his head spinning from how fast this day—their whole relationship—had fallen apart. "The sooner we cut ties, the better for us both."

Even though it hurt like hell.

And, in spite of everything, it damned well did. But trust was hard enough for him after how his father had betrayed the family, making a lie out of all the values he'd impressed on his kids. Cal couldn't live a lie any more than he could justify someone else's. It just wasn't who he wanted to be, even if the woman staring back at him was—he'd thought—the most incredible woman he'd ever met.

Apparently, the vision of her that he'd built in his head didn't match up with the real one.

Josie didn't say another word. She simply pivoted on her heel and headed for the stairs, a pack of worried animals following in her wake.

Kungfu stopped at the bottom of the steps to stare back at him. Waiting? Accusing?

But Cal didn't budge. Josie had come through Last Stand like a wrecking ball to everything that mattered to him, and the sooner she left, the better.

UPSTAIRS IN THE farmhouse, Josie packed her bag slowly, her suitcase orderly—her heart a shattered mess. If she could have gotten her things together faster, she would have, since it was obvious how much Cal wanted her gone. But her body felt uncoordinated, her limbs awkward and heavy, as she tried to fold things and organize her small suitcase.

Cal wanted her gone. The reality of that hurt her from her toes to the roots of her hair. Especially after the night they'd shared together.

She realized she'd folded the same blouse three times now. Somehow it kept ending up in her hands. It was like her brain had checked out on her—or maybe her thoughts were just too busy going over and over what she'd done wrong. Clearly, it had been foolish of her to think she could hide her head in the sand here, hoping things would settle down back home with her mother. Josie knew now she should have followed up on her mother's threats. Hiding out in a different state with a different phone number only made her look more guilty. She should have turned herself in and asked for a public defender to help her articulate her side.

Because, damn it, she felt like she'd done the best she could under impossible circumstances. She just hadn't counted on Cal getting caught up in her drama. She hadn't wanted his career to suffer because of her.

After grabbing her toiletries from the bathroom, she

dried off her shampoo bottle and stuck it in her bag, uncertain what she should have done differently. Should she have turned in her own mother for poor management? For not upholding her obligations to her tenants? Probably. But, like Cal, she'd been performing to a parent's expectations since well before she turned eighteen. So by the time she'd come of age, it had been hard to walk away from the things she'd always done to help tenants.

She'd felt needed. The people who lived in the building had appreciated her. And that had been...nice. What hadn't been nice? Keeping her past a secret from Cal. She hadn't realized how much he deserved to know about it until things unfolded in the kitchen. His career was on the line right now, and she'd risked that.

And she'd seen the betrayal in his eyes. Pain twisted inside her. She couldn't think about that moment—about him and all they'd lost—or she wouldn't be able to keep moving.

Scanning the room to see what else she might have forgotten, Josie's gaze fell on a framed family photograph from a long-ago Peach Festival. The three Ramsey brothers stood in the background while that year's Peach Queen—their younger sister—received her crown. Hailey Decker stood on one side of her sons, all her attention on her daughter's moment in the spotlight. But Clint Ramsey flanked the boys on the opposite end, and his attention was on Cal, who seemed to be the recipient of a lecture since Clint's mouth was open and he was gesturing with his hands.

All three of Clint's sons looked at their father.

What a telling family moment. A tiny piece of visual evidence for the kind of childhood Josie had only heard about in small doses. The expectations for the Ramsey sons were high, and the importance of their achievements overshadowed the teenaged daughter's. Worse, the boys had been dialed in to their father's world so thoroughly they didn't have time for anything else. Not even celebrating their sister's moment in the spotlight.

Was it any wonder Cal couldn't forgive Josie when her secrets threatened the only thing that mattered to this family? Cal had been on a path of his father's choosing since he was a child, and now she'd cost him his dream.

Defeat sighed over her.

Shouldering her backpack, she zipped her suitcase and headed downstairs. She didn't see Cal in the kitchen anymore, although the remains of their breakfast were gone, the dishes washed and dried. There was no trace of their time together. Out the window, she saw him in the backyard, on the phone near his car. Was he going to try and escort her to the town line? Boot her out as soon as they crossed it?

The resentful thoughts dissipated as her gaze lingered on his face. His brows were drawn together, his shoulders taut as he rubbed one hand along the back of his neck. The distress in his expression was clear, and she was responsible for causing it. Knowing she'd hurt him stabbed right through her, causing a far worse pain than any fear she felt for her future. Her regret was even deeper than the pain she felt in losing him—and that was saying a whole lot, because walking away from Calvin Ramsey was going to be far more painful than the hurt and humiliation she'd felt over finding out Tom Belvedere had pulled the wool over her eyes.

With Cal, it was so much different. Tom scraped her pride but not her heart. Whereas the feelings she had for Cal were going to break her in two if she didn't leave fast. Not caring if she was ten times a coward, she would make her escape out the front door where he wouldn't see her. She couldn't bear to witness the cold distance in his eyes again.

Besides, there was nothing left to say.

Swallowing the lump in her throat, she gave one last head scratch to each of the dogs and kissed all their furry heads, then headed outdoors into the hot Texas day. She hadn't checked the bus schedule, but she had plenty of time to figure out her next move on the long walk to the nearest stop for public transportation. First and foremost, she planned to phone the sheriff's department in her hometown and find out what kind of mess she was facing legally.

As much as she didn't want to return to Florida, she must need to appear in court. She only hoped she hadn't missed a date already.

Withdrawing her phone from her pocket, she noticed her fingers were shaking as she pulled up the screen to dial. Then she remembered she didn't know the number. She paused on the gravel road to search for the number online, knowing she might not have Wi-Fi again for a while and she hadn't paid the extra money for data on her cheap cell. She was still close enough to the house to get a search result. Tapping the number for the sheriff's department, Josie took a deep breath when someone answered.

"Hello." Her voice wavered more than her trembling hands. "I think I need to turn myself in."

Chapter Eleven

C AL WANDERED AROUND the backyard while he waited for Josie to emerge from the house, knowing he at least owed her a ride to wherever she wanted to go next. He tried not to think about that, knowing he was leaving her in a difficult position since she hadn't made plans beyond this job. Then again, maybe she had. It had become glaringly apparent today that he didn't know everything about Josie Vance.

And that hurt so much more than it should have based on how long they'd known one another. He'd fallen hard and fast for her, in a relationship far different from any in his past. Finding out he'd fallen for a lie made every moment painful since he'd read that photo caption.

The sun beat down with a relentless heat, so he kept to the shade as much as possible, weaving from one hickory tree to another until he reached the beehives. He should check them to make sure he knew how to care for them until his mother returned from her trip, but once he stood near the simple wood-frame structures, he realized there was a lot he didn't understand. Bees worked tirelessly, flying in and out of their home base, while Cal tried to remember what Josie had told him about them. Should he check on the colonies that she'd brought over to Rough Hollow Orchards for his grandfather?

Withdrawing his phone, he texted his mother to call him the next time she had phone service. He owed her a personal heads-up about Josie. About the past she'd hidden. He jabbed the send button on the message. When his mother got back to him, he'd ask her about the bees. That done, he tried to quell his emotions by losing himself in taking care of business. He sent a message to his agent to ask for help navigating the inevitable P.R. fallout that would come from being photographed with Josie. It was hardly a crime for him to socialize with a woman who was being criminally investigated. But it was exactly the kind of publicity that Dusty Reed didn't want near his team.

And even that didn't matter to Cal as much as being taken for a fool by someone he'd thought he cared about.

His phone rang as he hit send on the message to his agent, and Cal was surprised to see his mother's number.

"Mom?" He moved away from the bees toward the converted pole barn where an overhead fan spun lazily above a small patio table.

"Hello, Cal," his mother greeted him, the warmth and happiness in her voice sounding close enough to be in the next town and not a half of a world away. "I just happened to see your text while I'm in town doing some shopping. Is everything okay there?"

They hadn't spoken on the phone in months, but they'd

messaged since he'd returned to Last Stand. She knew he was checking on Everett and making some repairs around the farm while he stayed in the garage apartment, but she didn't know he'd fallen for Josie.

Of course, he'd only just realized that at the game the night before when he'd kissed Josie. The ache of how fast things had fallen apart still threatened to level him.

"Gramp is doing well enough," he assured her. "I just wanted to warn you that things didn't work out with...the caretaker." Saying her name aloud wasn't an option, not when he needed to keep his emotions out of the conversation. "I had to let her go."

A beat of silence passed before his mother spoke.

"Do you mean *my* caretaker? Josie?" She sounded alarmed.

"It's okay, Mom. I'm going to watch over things here," he rushed to reassure her. "I'll take care of everything until you return."

In the background of the call, he could hear a high-pitched horn sounding, and animal noises that might have been goats or sheep.

"Cal, where is Josie now?" she asked, a hint of exasperation creeping into her voice. "What do you mean you let her go?"

The heat was frying him even in the shade with a ceiling fan, so he headed back toward the farmhouse, wondering what could be taking Josie so long. Needing to put this behind him before she had the chance to shred his heart any further.

"I mean she's under criminal investigation, Mom." He mopped a hand over his forehead as he climbed the steps to the back porch, the anger, frustration and hurt climbing right along with him. "You really need to do background checks when you're hiring someone from outside the area—"

"So you *fired* her?" His mother sounded outright indignant, her voice rising while the sheep or goats or whatever continued to make a ruckus around her.

Shoving open the door to the house, he stepped inside the air conditioning to wait for Josie.

"She could have a warrant out for her arrest, Mom," he explained gently, knowing his mother only ever saw the best in people. "She was doing illegal contracting work—"

"I know, Cal," his mother cut him off with a hint of impatience. "I hired her as a favor to my friend who lives in the building she manages."

Dropping into a seat at the kitchen island, he tried to absorb that news.

"You knew?" Even so, that didn't reconcile the fact Josie hadn't been truthful with him about her past. And it sure as hell didn't salvage the fact that Cal's reputation would suffer at a time when he needed to keep his nose clean.

"Rita Gonzalez is the most kindhearted woman I met on last year's mission trip." More honking echoed in the background of her call. "So when she asked me about giving the young woman a job, I was happy to help. According to Rita, Josie takes good care of everyone in that building, people who wouldn't have any kind of help otherwise."

Cal's temples throbbed harder, trying to put the pieces together. "You knowingly hired someone who was under investigation in another state?"

"There were no charges against her at the time, Cal." His mom exchanged words with someone on her end, but he couldn't discern what she was saying. Besides, he was too blown away by the knowledge that his mother had been perfectly aware of Josie's background. When his mother returned to the call, she said, "Our bus is heading back to the village now, but it would mean a lot to me if you would assure Josie she can stay at the house until I return home. Whatever charges come up in Florida aren't going to stick without getting her mother in significant trouble, too. You realize it's her mother who is causing her all the grief, don't you?"

Pulling himself out of the chair, he peered up the staircase to listen for Josie. What was taking her so long up there?

Cal couldn't follow his mother's logic since the problem seemed clear-cut to him. Josie had broken the law. End of story. Just like in baseball, the rules of life were clear. They were written down, and they applied to everyone.

"Mom, if she's committed a crime—"

"She will get an attorney and argue her side," his mother retorted with a sigh. "The bus is leaving now, but please keep in mind not everything is black and white, Cal. Sometimes doing the right thing—the ethical, moral right thing—puts a person in a difficult position. I believe Rita that Josie is a very good person who did her best in a difficult situation."

In the background, Cal could hear the rumble of a diesel engine right before he lost the cell signal entirely.

Had he made the wrong decision to ask Josie to leave? His mother was one of the best people he knew. She'd taken the high road with Clint during their divorce, never bad-mouthing their father for his choices, and letting Clint's behavior speak for itself—in public and in private with their family.

He trusted his mom's moral compass as much as any-one's and she'd been quick to defend Josie. The hell of that was, she didn't even know Josie half as well as Cal did. The realization felt deflating. He'd seen what a good person Josie was with his own eyes. She'd kept track of Everett before Cal arrived home, visiting with him to talk about gardening. Baking him a pie. Studying how bees could best help the Rough Hollow crops and then ensuring the bees were delivered.

"Josie?" he called up the stairs to her now, needing to talk to her as he should have done before rather than just storming out.

Regretting that he'd been so rigid in his thinking, writing her off as a criminal for acts his mother considered "ethical and moral." Was he that blind?

The answer hurt to consider.

When she didn't answer, he pounded up the steps, need-ing to see her. Apologize for leaping to conclusions without listening to her side, really listening.

But once he was upstairs he knew right away she was gone. The dogs lay on the floor of the guest room where she'd stayed, as if waiting for her to return. Their heads popped up as he stepped over the threshold, tails wagging hopefully.

"Where did she go?" He turned back into the hall and that's when he saw two figures standing on the gravel road outside.

Josie wore a backpack, her rolling suitcase at her feet. Beside her, a more stooped figure with a walker, his bathrobe and slippers too warm for the hot summer day. Everett Ramsey appeared to be giving her a stern lecture, standing between her and the road out of Rough Hollow.

Cal took the steps two at a time, all three dogs at his heels. On a mission.

Thanks to his grandfather, Cal might still have a second shot with the woman he loved.

STILL STUNNED FROM her phone call to the sheriff's office, Josie was caught off guard when Everett Ramsey planted himself between her and her only escape route away from Cal.

Away from too many happy memories of their time together. Her heart was breaking, and she didn't want to fall apart in front of Cal's grandfather. The hurt was so much worse than when her last boyfriend had ripped her off.

"Everett, I told you, Cal's made up his mind, and he wants me to leave," Josie informed the older man a second time, not wanting to argue in the driveway.

The sun was too intense this time of day. She worried about Everett's health. Bad enough he pushed the walker on the uneven terrain every day. But the heat couldn't be good for him either, especially with all the clothes he piled on his thinning frame.

The older man had caught up to her while she'd been on the phone with the sheriff's department, and he seemed determined not to move.

"And I told *you*, my grandson's being a damned fool." Everett punctuated the words by pounding the heel of his fist on the rubber grip to his walker. "But I promise you this, he doesn't mean it."

"I should have been honest with him." She understood that now. Cal wasn't the kind of person who made do with half measures, the way she had her whole life.

He needed the whole picture to make informed decisions, and she'd robbed him of the ability to decide whether she was a good person or not. She couldn't escape the fact that she had broken the law. She knew his image was important to him and she'd knowingly put that at risk by keeping the truth from him. By withholding the truth and hoping for the best, she'd given him the worst possible view of her.

Cal did things the right way. With integrity and honesty. Everett shook his head so hard that a wisp of gray hair dislodged from the comb-over to stick straight up. "You've showed us nothing but kindness, my dear. If I knew nothing else about you, that would be enough."

The words were so sweetly unexpected, so thoughtful, they brought a tear to her eye. But then, her emotions were tumbling all over the place like a payload that wasn't tethered to the truck bed.

"Thank you, Everett," she whispered, her eyes going to his.

But he looked past her, at a spot over her shoulder.

Even as she turned, she heard dogs barking. Guessed that Cal must be heading their way. Her heart sank because she didn't think she could face him again. Not now when she was holding herself together with duct tape and string.

A typical Josie Vance patch job.

Cal's voice sounded behind her. "Gramp, it looks like one of the nurses is flagging you down to return to the house."

Josie turned to see a slim blonde in navy-blue scrubs hurrying their way. It was easier to focus on the aide than to look at Cal. Especially since she had wanted to leave without another confrontation.

"I wouldn't be out here now if you handled your business right the first time," Everett grumbled, shooting a glare at his grandson as he pushed his walker back toward his house. The older man paused as he passed Josie, his eyes kind. "Just know that if it was up to me, you wouldn't be leaving."

He covered her hand with his weathered one, squeezing with surprising strength before he continued toward the house. The aide was already reaching him, supervising the rest of his walk. From several yards away, Josie could hear him tell her he didn't need a babysitter.

A smile pulled at her lips even as another tear leaked free. She dashed it away and braced herself before turning to face Cal again.

His expression was less rigid than she remembered. Less angry. He sounded almost concerned when he spoke to her.

"I planned to drive you wherever you wanted to go," he chided her as he gestured to her suitcase, his T-shirt pulling tight around his biceps. "I was out back waiting for you."

His proximity shouldn't affect her, but she found herself remembering the ways they'd touched each other the night before. How happy she'd been this morning when she'd stepped into the kitchen. But that was in the past and she refused to let his tone fool her now. She couldn't let her guard down around him again.

Ever.

"You told me to leave. I took you at your word." She bent to pick up Kungfu, comforted by seeing her canine friends again.

"I'd never expect you to walk in this heat." He grabbed the suitcase handle and dragged it closer. "Let's talk inside."

She dug her heels in despite the heat, because her pride was all she had left now. "You were very clear that there was nothing more to say."

"I was wrong." He kept hold of her suitcase and reached for the strap on her backpack. "And you can't leave until we discuss it."

He was wrong? She wondered what that was all about. But the possibility of his hand grazing her arm was enough to get her moving. She couldn't risk a touch that might undermine all her mental defenses. It rattled her to realize how much she still wanted to lean in to him. To take shelter in his arms.

"I'll carry it." She shifted away from his outstretched fingers, but since he seemed determined to keep her suitcase captive, she followed him back to the farmhouse, her heart filling with a wary hope.

The heat decreased once they were under the shade of the big hickory trees that framed the yard, but Cal didn't stop walking until they were inside the front parlor of the farmhouse, a formal living area with windows overlooking the lawn. She was surprised he didn't keep moving to the backyard where his car waited, but she was too grateful for the blast of air conditioning to argue at the moment.

After setting down Kungfu, she slid off her backpack and waited for whatever he seemed determined to say. She stood in the foyer, hardwood creaking softly under her feet as she shifted her weight. Cal stalked deeper into the house, but then, as if noticing she didn't follow him, he closed the distance between them again. Stopping only a few feet from her in the foyer.

"First of all, I made a snap judgment of you this morning, and I'm sorry for that." His opening surprised her, but there was no denying that he was serious about the words. His green eyes were clear, his gaze direct.

Josie didn't know what to make of it, but he definitely had her attention.

"I should have told you the truth. I knew your career was important to you—that your image was important to you—and I've put both at risk." The fault was hers. She'd been scared to show him her past, and it had hurt him.

She would always regret that.

"But I could have at least listened to you this morning. Learned the whole story." He seemed frustrated as he swiped a hand through his dark hair and paced away from her again. "Instead, I shut down, rooted in my own thinking."

"Because you had every reason to be angry with me," she assured him, hating that she'd brought the dark cloud of her problems to cast shadows over the life he'd built.

"That doesn't mean I shouldn't have heard you out. My whole life, I've gravitated to baseball because it was always so much more comprehensible than my real life." He wandered into the parlor where the walls were lined with old family photos and framed news articles about Ramsey successes. He stopped in front of a headline about Wes getting drafted. "There are clearly defined metrics, so you know how you're doing. Success is weighed by your stats, not the fickle affections of a parent who pushed me with one hand and undermined me with the other."

The muscle in his jaw flexed as he moved on to straighten a photo of Nate with a championship team.

She followed him into the parlor, saying nothing since she wasn't sure where all this was headed. But she listened, because she was curious about what was going on in his head even if there was no room for her in his heart or his life.

"But maybe I got a little too comfortable with letting baseball be the model for my life. I sure haven't been a presence in my family for a long time, and there's no excuse for me not knowing about Gramp's accident." He shook his head and moved away from the old photos, walking across the bright braided rug toward her again. "I've been seeing the world in black and white, simplifying everything down to quantifiable terms, even though that doesn't work for every situation in life."

"Like mine?"

She hadn't meant to say it aloud. But the words echoed in her ears, magnified in her mind because it felt so significant to think maybe Cal understood a little bit.

"Exactly." He stopped near her, all that strength and male vitality close enough to touch. "I judged you too quickly, based on too little information, because I was worried about my own career. My own image."

The hurt in his eyes, his disappointment in himself, was easy to see before he hung his head.

"I've tried hard to be a different man than my father," he continued, his voice deeper now, hinting at the raw emotions behind the words. "But today I behaved the way he would— more concerned for myself than other people around me.

Someone I care about."

The last part caught her off guard.

Her heartbeat stuttered.

Cal had said he was wrong. Had he changed his mind about her? About them? She had warned herself not to let her guard down, but the possibility of salvaging their fledging relationship tugged at her heart.

"I don't want to misunderstand." She felt shaky, her hand reaching for the back of the sofa to steady her. "What are you saying, Cal?"

"I'm saying that I was wrong to judge you and I'm more sorry than you can imagine." He took her hand lightly in his, stroking his thumb along the backs of her knuckles. "I hope you can forgive me, Josie, but if you can't I understand. Either way, please know that my mother may never forgive me for firing you, so it would mean a lot to me if you'd stay on as caretaker until she gets back."

"You told your mother about my…circumstances?" Anxiety sent a nervous tremble through her. She owed Hailey Decker an apology, regretted taking advantage of such a kind woman.

Josie tugged her hand away from Cal's, even though his touch had been the nicest thing to happen to her since their argument earlier. She didn't deserve it.

"She already knew," Cal informed her, surprising her. "Apparently she's friends with one of the women in your building—"

"Mrs. Gonzalez." The pieces fell into place for her as

soon as Cal started. "She's the one who urged me to answer your mother's ad in the first place. First, she showed me the ad online, then she gave me the bus fare money to get here since I was flat broke."

She couldn't believe the kindness of both women. Rita Gonzalez, for doing all she could to help Josie extricate herself from her job, and Hailey Decker for taking a chance on Josie based on a friend's word. Josie might have an extremely difficult relationship with her mother, but she didn't lack for wonderful mother figures with those kinds of women in her corner. Their efforts to help her touched her more than she could say. But the guilt lingered, because she really wished she'd been honest with Cal's mother from the start.

She needed to start trusting in people again, start trusting in her own self-worth too, so she didn't land in the messes she had in the past.

"I hate that you felt like you didn't have any options, that you couldn't just quit your job with your mother and find work that would make you happy somewhere else." Cal's touch returned, and he brushed a caress along her arm. "But selfishly, I'm glad that it brought you here. And I still really wish you'd stay and finish out the job here."

This time, she allowed herself to feel the draw of his hand on her. Letting it persuade her. But she wanted so much more than just the security of this job.

She wanted Cal.

"I won't regret my time in Last Stand," she assured him,

trying to find the right way to track back to their earlier conversation, when he'd said he was sorry for judging her. Did he mean that he regretted ending things? Or just that he regretted the harshness of *how* he'd ended them? The warmth of his fingers on her forearm gave her reason to hope. "And I'll stay to finish the job if it's just the same with you. The sheriff's office back home told me I can go into a local police office to give a statement in response to the citation against me, so I don't need to go home right away." The legalese confused her, but the officer she spoke to had been both helpful and reassuring, suggesting the charges would never stick if she hadn't been compensated for the work. And she hadn't—she'd never made a dime above her regular salary as a building supervisor. "But I don't want my presence to cause more trouble for you and your family."

"I'd like you to stay," he told her firmly, bracketing her shoulders between his palms. Steadying her. "More than that, I want you in my life any way I can have you." He waited, as if letting the words sink in.

She couldn't answer, shock robbing her of words.

Last night, she'd felt the same way, but things had changed so quickly today. She tracked his movements as he reached to cup her face, tilting her chin toward him.

Could they really still have a chance together?

"I'm uncertain of my career," Cal admitted, his voice rumbling from his chest to hers, vibrating through her. "But I'm not willing to give you up to please a manager, so whatever comes I'll handle it. I know it's not fair to ask you for a future when I don't know what that might look like, but I am willing to compromise to find a way we can be happy together." The sincerity in his words and in his gaze was unmistakable. "That is, if you'll still have me."

Chapter Twelve

"YES." NODDING, SHE tried to clear her throat gone raspy from emotions. "I want you in my life, too."

Happiness made her knees weak as they stood together in the front room of the farmhouse, an old-fashioned cuckoo clock chiming the hour as the afternoon wore on.

"Does that mean you can forgive me for this morning?" Cal asked, studying her expression as if searching for any hidden reservations. "I'm sorry I was so quick to judge you."

His words went a long way to heal the hurt she'd felt earlier.

"I forgive you, Cal. If you don't protect your image and your reputation, who will? I should have told you up front about the circumstances that made me leave Florida." Josie wrapped her arms around Cal, holding him close for a long moment. "I've been dealing with my mother for so long that I was just happy to forget it all for a while and bury my head in the sand. But you deserved better."

She felt the tension in him ease in a shuddering breath, and it touched her to know how much her forgiveness meant. How much she meant.

She'd never had a love like that. Now, more than anything, she wanted to protect and nurture the gift of that kind of love.

"No more secrets," he promised her. "From now on, there's no quota on how many questions we ask each other."

She smiled against his shoulder before easing away to look up at him. "Okay. Why don't you start by asking me where things stand with the charges against me?"

He frowned, but his palms on her back rubbed warm circles. Comforting. Understanding.

"Where do things stand, Josie? We'll get you the best attorney to fight this."

She appreciated his unconditional support so much. She could get used to having a partner who believed in her, who would help her when things got difficult. But in return, she needed to be that kind of stabilizing presence for him as well, to support him when his career was rocky, or when his dad tried to undermine all the great things he'd achieved.

"I phoned the sheriff's office to turn myself in and—first and foremost—I got some good news."

His eyebrows shot up as he drew her to sit on the sofa beside him. "You did?"

"The officer I spoke to is the same one who investigated the con artist who swindled me, and would you believe they arrested him *and* recovered almost all of my savings?" She'd been stunned when she'd heard. Of course, the police hadn't been able to inform her because she'd left town and changed phone numbers in her ill-conceived effort to hide from her past. "It wasn't all that much money, but it's everything I had. And they got back ninety percent of what I'd lost."

The money was the least of what she'd won today, but she was still glad to have her savings returned to her.

Cal wrapped her in his strong arms. Squeezing. "That's excellent news. I hope the bastard does some jail time."

She took comfort from the hug as much as the words. She was so grateful to have this second chance with him.

"He will. I wasn't the first of his victims, so there are quite a few charges, apparently." She edged back on the deep cushion to peer up into his eyes. "But the other good news is that the photo caption about me being under investigation was misleading."

"Really?" He sounded skeptical.

"My mother wanted to press charges against me, but since she was employing me, she couldn't provide evidence of my wrongdoing without seriously implicating herself." Maybe a better daughter would feel badly about that. But Josie's sympathies were with the tenants who'd had to put up with poor conditions too often over the years. "When Mom tried to backpedal, the state's housing assistance authorities got involved. So technically, I do need to give a formal statement, but the ultimate investigation isn't about me. It's my mother's business that is under state scrutiny."

She could see now that she'd given her mother far too much space in her head, believing her to have a level of smarts and power that she didn't. The fact that her mom had gotten herself into legal trouble in an effort to be vindictive with Josie—that was all the proof she needed that her mom wasn't as sharp as she'd given her credit for.

He nodded, seeming to think it over. "We should still send you in there with a good attorney to make sure you're protected."

"Thank you." She appreciated the thought. And the help. No doubt she should have reported her mother long ago, but underneath all the difficult, convoluted feelings she had for her mom, she loved her.

In the future, she would need to draw better boundaries if she ever resumed a relationship with her, but for now, Josie felt grateful to have a life of her own. A future that could include Cal.

Most of all, she was so glad to know that he was beside her from this day forward. She wondered how she'd gotten so lucky to have him in her life. A man of Calvin Ramsey's principles would never change his mind about this. About her.

The giddiness of the joy made her light-headed as he pulled her against him again.

"I should message my agent to update him about that situation," Cal said softly against her hair as he kissed the top of her head. "But before I do that, I think we should talk about what happens next for us. Because nothing's more important, or more pressing, than making sure you know how much I care for you."

Her feelings bloomed like a spring garden, filling her up. She glanced up at him.

"I feel the same way." She didn't want to hide the truth

of her emotions, even if Cal didn't return them yet. "I'm in love with you, Cal. That's why it pained me so much to know how deeply I'd hurt you."

He cradled her face in his hands, a new tenderness in his gaze.

"I love you, Josie. If I didn't feel that way about you, today wouldn't have hurt so damned much in the first place." He kissed one cheek, and then the other. "But I don't want to think about what went wrong anymore. I want to focus on the future. Together."

Her heart overflowed with happiness. With love.

"I'd like that, too." Tears stung her eyes to think about how lucky she was to have a second chance at this. To be with someone who could forgive the mistakes she'd made. "So much."

"But what if I get a call to join a team tomorrow?" he asked, studying her carefully. "Will you be happy following me around the country while I play? Would you like a home base in Last Stand? Or in whatever city my team is based in?"

"I want to be wherever you are, as often as that's possible." She felt like the whole world was opening up to her. "But I could be very happy in Last Stand whenever we can be here."

She would like getting to know his mother better. Spending more time with Everett or helping out at the farm.

"I want to spend more time here, too. If I don't hear from a team, I'd be ready to build a home for us this summer."

"But I'm going to hope that you get a call." She didn't want to start their future together with the cloud of how she'd possibly tainted his image hanging over them.

"My record speaks for itself," he assured her. "Either they want me or they don't, and I'm going to be okay with that." He stroked a stay hair behind her ear. "I mean it. I just want you to be happy, Josie." He leaned closer, and this time his lips slanted across hers for a long, lingering kiss. "All the time."

"I know one surefire thing that would make me happy," she confessed, her body coming alive under his touch. "And when you kiss me that way, I can't think about anything else."

Cal's soft laugh sent a different kind of pleasure through her. A certainty that they could make this work. A confidence that they could carry each other through whatever the future might bring.

"In this case, maybe we should table the rest of this discussion until we celebrate everything we've figured out so far. I don't want you to be too distracted to focus." He slid his hands around her waist, tunneling under her T-shirt. "You think some time under the sheets will help take the edge off?"

"I do." Already, her breath came faster, need for this man setting her fingers in motion to explore the hard planes of his body. "After the emotional roller coaster of this morning, I feel like we need to hit the reset button. Start with sex. End with pie. Solve the world's problems in between."

Cal didn't laugh this time. He was already carrying her toward the staircase, his expression intent. For her part, Josie wrapped her arms around him and held on tight, very ready to celebrate a new beginning.

The End

If you enjoyed *The Perfect Catch*,
you'll love the next books in...

The Texas Playmakers series

Book 1: *The Perfect Catch*
Calvin Ramsey's story

Book 2: *Coming soon*
Nate Ramsey's story

Book 3: *Coming soon*
Wes Ramsey's story

Available now at your favorite online retailer!

Don't miss more by Joanne Rock

The Road to Romance Series

When a popular life coach claims that making peace with
your romantic past paves the way for romance in the future,
the idea inspires a group of down-on-their-luck friends to
follow the advice. As they set out to sever ties with the past,
they are each surprised to find sexy adventure along the way!

Book 1: *Last Chance Christmas*

Book 2: *Second Chance Cowboy*

Book 3: *A Chance This Christmas*

Available now at your favorite online retailer!

About the Author

Joanne Rock writes romance of all shapes and sizes from sexy contemporary to medieval historical and an occasional Young Adult story. She's penned over seventy books, appearing most often in the Harlequin Blaze series. Joanne taught English at the college level before becoming a full-time writer, and she returns to the classroom as often as possible to share her love of stories. A quiet and unassuming Virgo, Joanne married a fiery and boisterous Aries man in true opposites-attract fashion. Visit her website at www.JoanneRock.com.

Thank you for reading

The Perfect Catch

If you enjoyed this book, you can find more from all our great authors at TulePublishing.com, or from your favorite online retailer.

TULE
PUBLISHING